ADVENTURES IN THE RIFLE BRIGADE. First printing. July 2016. ISBN: 978-1-63215-802-4. Published by Image Comics, Inc. Office of publication: 2001 Center Street, Sixth Floor, Berkeley, CA 94704. Contains material originally published in single magazine form as ADVENTURES IN THE RIFLE BRIGADE #1-3, and ADVENTURES IN THE RIFLE BRIGADE: OPERATION BOLLOCK #1-3.

GARTH ENNIS
WRITER

CARLOS EZQUERRA
ARTIST

PATRICIA MULVIHILL KEVIN SOMERS
COLORISTS

CLEM ROBBINS
LETTERER

BRIAN BOLLAND GLENN FABRY
ORIGINAL SERIES COVERS

CREATED BY
GARTH ENNIS
AND
CARLOS EZQUERRA

DEDICATION

To the writers, artists and editorial staff of

Battle Picture Weekly
Warlord
Battle Picture Library
War Picture Library
and *Commando*

With the utmost affection and respect.
— GARTH ENNIS

BOLLAND

FOUR MILES OVER BERLIN, JUNE 1944:
I BROKE UP WITH MY GIRLFRIEND LAST WEEK...
ONCE MORE UNTO THE BREACH

I SAY, NOT HAVING MUCH LUCK WITH THE POPSIES, ARE YOU, OLD BOY? THAT'S THE THIRD ONE GONE FOR A BURTON THIS YEAR!
THIRD ONE THIS MONTH, ACTUALLY, SIR.

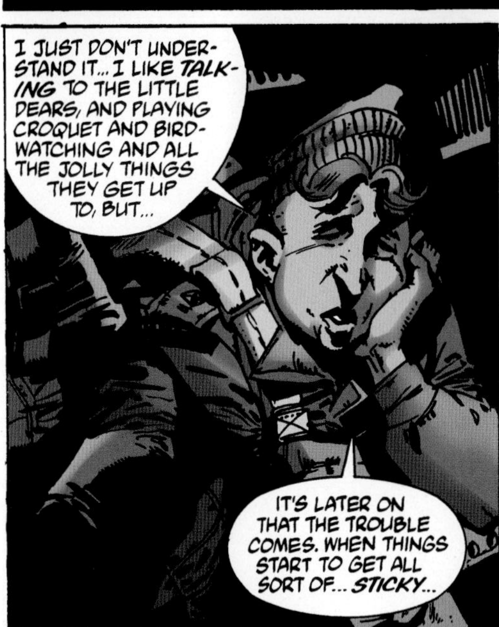
I JUST DON'T UNDERSTAND IT... I LIKE *TALKING* TO THE LITTLE DEARS, AND PLAYING CROQUET AND BIRD-WATCHING AND ALL THE JOLLY THINGS THEY GET UP TO, BUT...
IT'S LATER ON THAT THE TROUBLE COMES. WHEN THINGS START TO GET ALL SORT OF... *STICKY*...

WELL, NEVER MIND! COMMANDO MISSIONS ARE MUCH MORE FUN THAN GIRLS ANYWAY!
YOU WAIT AND SEE: YOU'LL SLIT SOME BUGGER'S THROAT OPEN, BLOW UP A BRIDGE OR TWO, PUMP HOT LEAD INTO A SQUAD OF SCREAMING JERRIES--AND BEFORE YOU KNOW IT, YOU'LL BE RIGHT AS RAIN AGAIN...

D'YOU REALLY THINK *SO!!*
GAD!

THAT'S *NOT* PLAYING THE GAME, FRITZ! WE AREN'T EVEN OUT OF THE BALLY AEROPLANE YET!

BLOODY CHEEK!
WHERE WAS I...?
L-LOOK HERE, SIR, IS THIS REALLY SUCH A GOOD IDEA? JUMPING INTO THE MIDDLE OF A-- A THOUSAND BOMBER RAID?
WELL, IT'S THE PERFECT COVER, ISN'T IT? JERRY'S NOT LIKELY TO BE LOOKING OUT FOR PARACHUTISTS ON A NIGHT LIKE THIS!
NO, HE'LL BE SKULKING IN HIS CELLAR WITH HIS SAUSAGE AND SAUERKRAUT! PROBABLY BEING BEASTLY TO A FRAULEIN WITHOUT THE BENEFIT OF BUTTER!
IF YOU SAY SO, SIR...
ABSOLUTELY! BE IN AND OUT BEFORE THEY KNOW WHAT'S HIT 'EM!
WHY, AT THIS PRECISE MOMENT I WOULDN'T CHANGE PLACES WITH ANYONE!
TOP SECRET MISSION TO SMITE THE KING'S ENEMIES--EXCELLENT CHANCE OF A GLORIOUS DEATH IN THE SERVICE OF ONE'S COUNTRY--LEADING A BUNCH OF WIZARD CHAPS--
THE FINEST FIGHTING MEN THE BRITISH ARMY CAN PRODUCE--
THE RIFLE BRIGADE!!

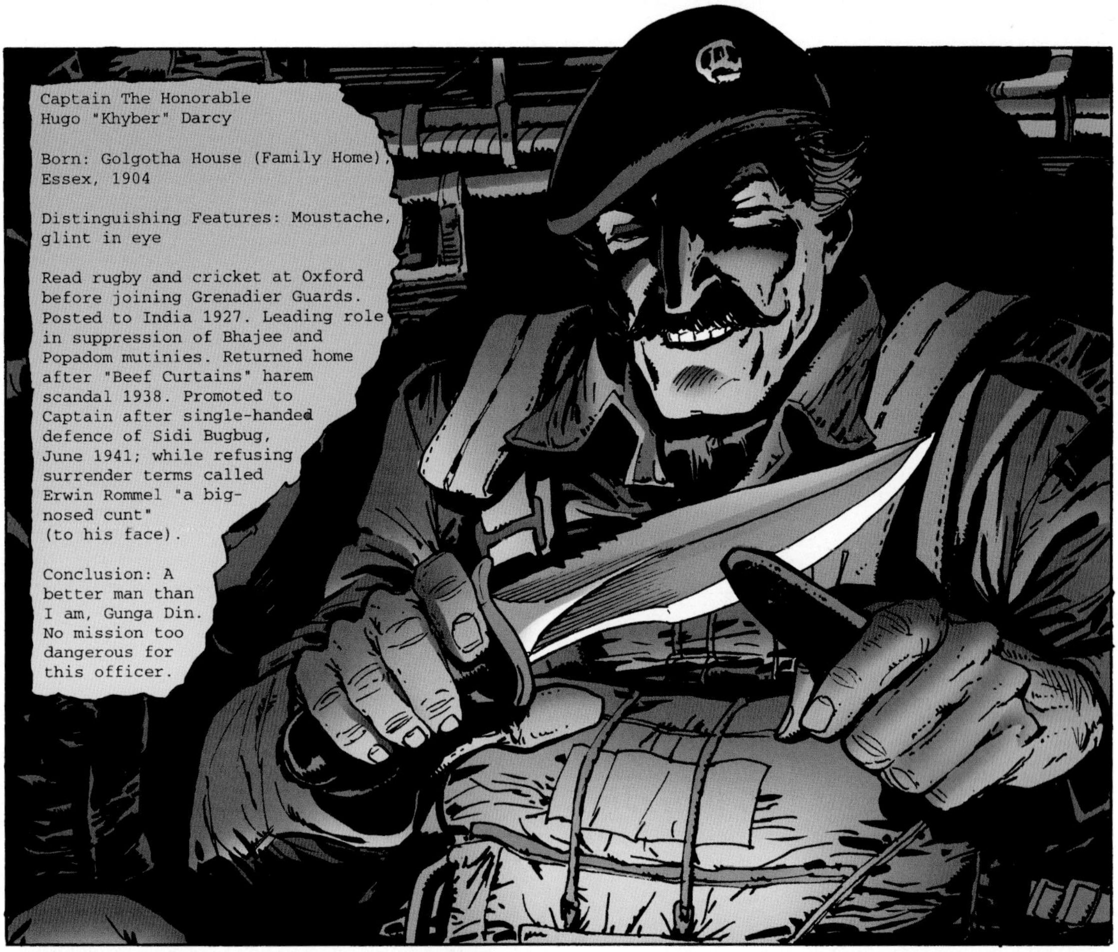

Captain The Honorable
Hugo "Khyber" Darcy

Born: Golgotha House (Family Home), Essex, 1904

Distinguishing Features: Moustache, glint in eye

Read rugby and cricket at Oxford before joining Grenadier Guards. Posted to India 1927. Leading role in suppression of Bhajee and Popadom mutinies. Returned home after "Beef Curtains" harem scandal 1938. Promoted to Captain after single-handed defence of Sidi Bugbug, June 1941; while refusing surrender terms called Erwin Rommel "a big-nosed cunt" (to his face).

Conclusion: A better man than I am, Gunga Din. No mission too dangerous for this officer.

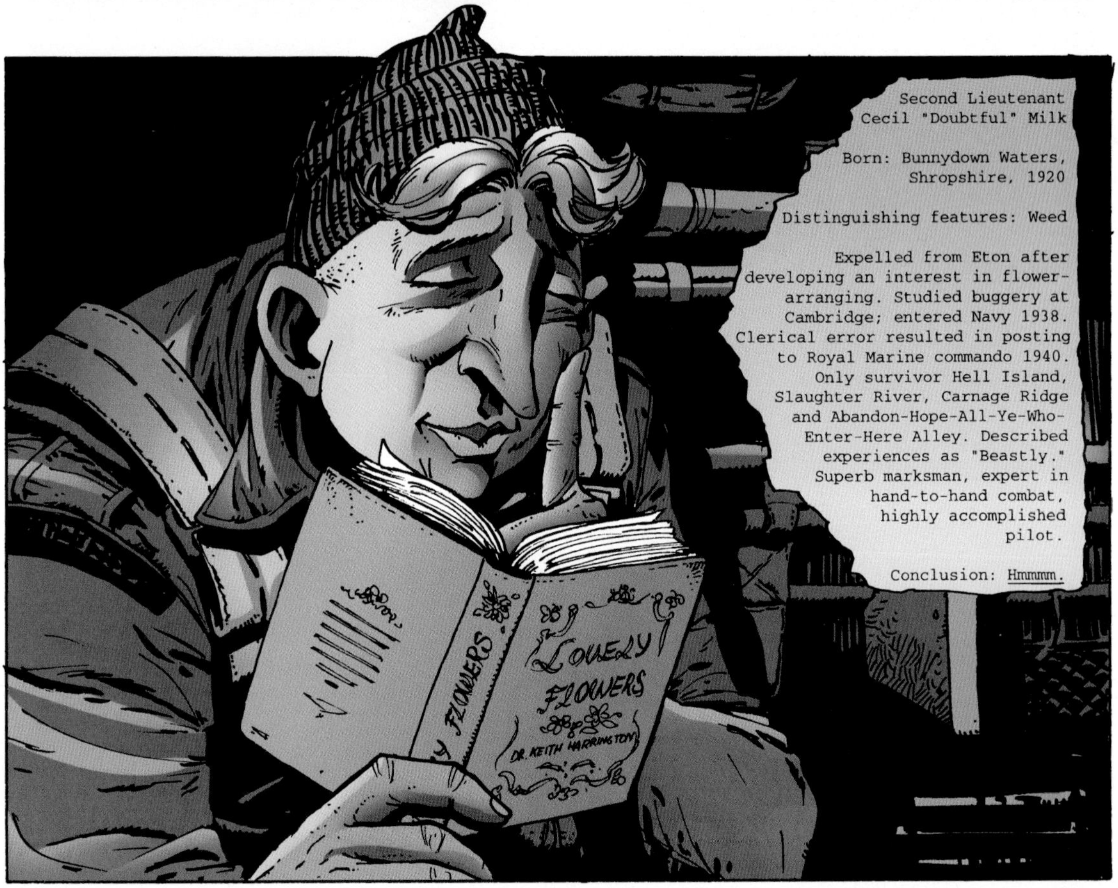

Second Lieutenant
Cecil "Doubtful" Milk

Born: Bunnydown Waters, Shropshire, 1920

Distinguishing features: Weed

Expelled from Eton after developing an interest in flower-arranging. Studied buggery at Cambridge; entered Navy 1938. Clerical error resulted in posting to Royal Marine commando 1940. Only survivor Hell Island, Slaughter River, Carnage Ridge and Abandon-Hope-All-Ye-Who-Enter-Here Alley. Described experiences as "Beastly." Superb marksman, expert in hand-to-hand combat, highly accomplished pilot.

Conclusion: Hmmmm.

EY-OOP!
Sergeant Crumb
Born: Thraip, East Yorkshire, 1908
Distinguishing features: largest man in British armed forces
Parents emigrated after birth. Institutionalised age one. Devoured Uncle. Served five of seven-year sentence after "Brick Shithouse" incident; fellow inmates of Chinnery Prison never found. Posted Rifle Brigade 3 Sept. '39. Expert neck-wringer.
Conclusion: I'm frightened, Mummy.
YER AHT OF ORDAH!
Corporal Geezer
Born: Butcher Lane, East London, 1920
Distinguishing features: Ghastly working class accent
Promoted from wretch to urchin 1927. Graduated early as Cut-throat thug 1935. Suspected of shouting "wanker" during Royal visit to East End slums but never convicted. Tried for 413 counts of murder; sentence waived on posting to Rifle Brigade 3 Sept '39.
Conclusion: Absolute rotter.
COMMANDOS

GAWD DAMMIT...
Hank the Yank
Born: The Colonies, 1914
Distinguishing features: Huge cigar and helmet, loudness
Arrived from Yankeeland 1940. Volunteered for active service before official U.S. declaration of war. Claimed would "show you tea-sipping Brits how it's done" as these people often do (no idea why, they weren't much use in the last show). Genius with explosives.
Conclusion: Typical bloody Yank, all mouth and trousers
The Piper
Born: The Fuckles, Glasgow, 1836
Distinguishing Features: Scottishness
Real name unknown. Came south from Ghillie Jocko land as youth; in service to Darcy family five wars and counting. Rarely speaks. Dark mutterings on record re."a braw bricht moonlicht nicht the nicht," also reference to "wee wifie waitin' at the aul' but an' ben". Top S.O.E. code-breakers baffled.
Conclusion: Mad as an otter.

GREEN LIGHT SHOWING! GO!

ALL RIGHT CHAPS, WE'RE ON! I'LL SEE YOU ALL SCHNITZEL-SIDE!
PIPER-- McAUGHTRY'S ARSE!

NYEEE-AIIII-HEEE-HI-HO-HAR
AARRRGH!!

HO-HAR
GERONIMO!!
AWFULLY SORRY, OLD BOY... THE FELLOWS LIKE IT, IT SEEMS TO BUCK THEM UP...
GOD! JUMP! JUST JUMP!

OH I SAY, I DON'T MUCH CARE FOR THIS...!
LOOK OUT ABOVE!

GAWD DAMMIT!
YER AHT OF ORDAH!!

TRIFLE WARM TONIGHT! THAT'S WHAT YOU GET FOR PLAYING WITH MATCHES, FRITZ!
TERRA FIRMA COMING UP, YOU CHAPS! KEEP AN EYE OUT FOR BROTHER BOCHE!

ALL RIGHT, QUICK AS YOU LIKE... ANYONE SEEN LIEUTENANT MILK?
DOUBTFUL! WHERE ARE YOU? SPEAK UP, OLD BOY!
H-HERE...!

NO!
TERRIBLY SORRY, SIR... THINK I STOPPED SOME SHRAPNEL ON THE WAY DOWN...

CHIN UP, DOUBTFUL! YOU'LL BE FINE!
IT'S ALL UP FOR ME, CAPTAIN DARCY...
I CAN SEE SOMETHING THROUGH THE MISTS... IS IT BLIGHTY, SIR? IS IT?

OH GOD, WHY, WHY? WHY COULDN'T IT HAVE BEEN ME? I'LL NEVER FORGIVE MYSELF!
THERE'S JUST... ONE THING YOU COULD DO FOR ME...

ANYTHING, DOUBTFUL! ANYTHING AT ALL, I SWEAR IT!
A-ANY-THING, SIR?
ON MY HONOR AS A GENTLE-MAN!

THEN KISS ME GOODNIGHT... CAPTAIN DARCY...

IT WOULD MEAN SO MUCH, SIR... A KISS BEFORE BEDTIME, LIKE NANNY USED TO DO...
THEN OUT, OUT, BRIEF CANDLE...
YES, BUT-- I MEAN HOLD ON, I--

YOU DID SAY ANYTHING...
BUT-- BUT--
ON YOUR HONOR, YOU SAID...

OH GOD.
THERE IS SOME CORNER OF A FOREIGN FIELD, THAT IS... FOREVER ENGLAND...
COMMANDOS

I SAY, JUST A MINUTE! THAT'S HARDLY EVEN A SCRATCH!

CRIKEY, NEITHER IT IS! AWFULLY SORRY, SIR, IT FELT HEAPS WORSE THAN IT LOOKS!
YES, WELL...
HMMM.

RIGHT, ah... FIRST THINGS FIRST. WE'RE NOT GOING TO GET VERY FAR IN KHAKI, SO KEEP AN EYE OUT FOR--
IT'S A LONG WAY TO MUNCHEN-GLADBACH... ♪

♪ IT'S A LONG WAY TO GO!
IT'S A LONG WAY TO MUNCHEN-GLADBACH, TO THE SWEETEST GIRL I KNOW! ♪

AUF WIEDERSEHEN, UNTER DEN LINDEN... GOODBYE ROSEN-STRASSE... ♪
WHERE IS ROSENSTRASSE, KARL? THIS SCHNAPPS IS LIKE BLOODY V-1 FUEL!
I THINK THE TOMMIES HAVE BOMBED IT FLAT, HANS. ACH, THE OLD TOWN'S NOT WHAT IT USED TO BE, IS IT?

NEIN, KARL, NEIN. ONCE I'D HAVE KILLED FOR A WEEK'S LEAVE IN BERLIN-- BUT NOW, WELL, IT'S HARDLY LIKELY TO HELP A MAN FORGET THE HORRORS OF THE RUSSIAN FRONT...
FOR MYSELF, I WISH ONLY TO RETURN TO MY LITTLE FARM IN THE ALPS--WITH HEIDI, AND LITTLE PAUL AND HEINRICH, AND MY FAITHFUL OLD HOUND WILLY...
ACH! I HAVE SO MUCH TO LIVE FOR!

WHAT ABOUT YOU, LADS? WOULDN'T YOU RATHER JUST GO HOME AND FORGET THE WHOLE VERDAMMT THING?

LADS?!
MEIN GOTT HANS, THE LADS ARE GONE! THEY MUST HAVE BEEN KILLED IN THE BOMBING!

HANS?!

BLAM
QUICK AS YOU CAN, CHAPS! QUIETLY DOES IT!

LOOK HERE, I REALLY AM TERRIBLY SORRY ABOUT THIS--
KRAK

EY-OOP!
SQUINCH

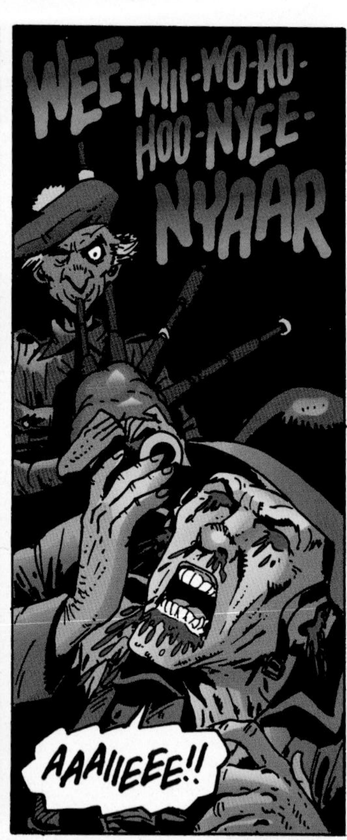

JUST THE TICKET! THE HUN WON'T SUSPECT A THING!

ON WITH THE SHOW, YOU CHAPS!

BIT OF A FLY IN THE OINTMENT HERE, SIR...
BUGGERATION! RATHER A LOT OF THE BLIGHTERS!

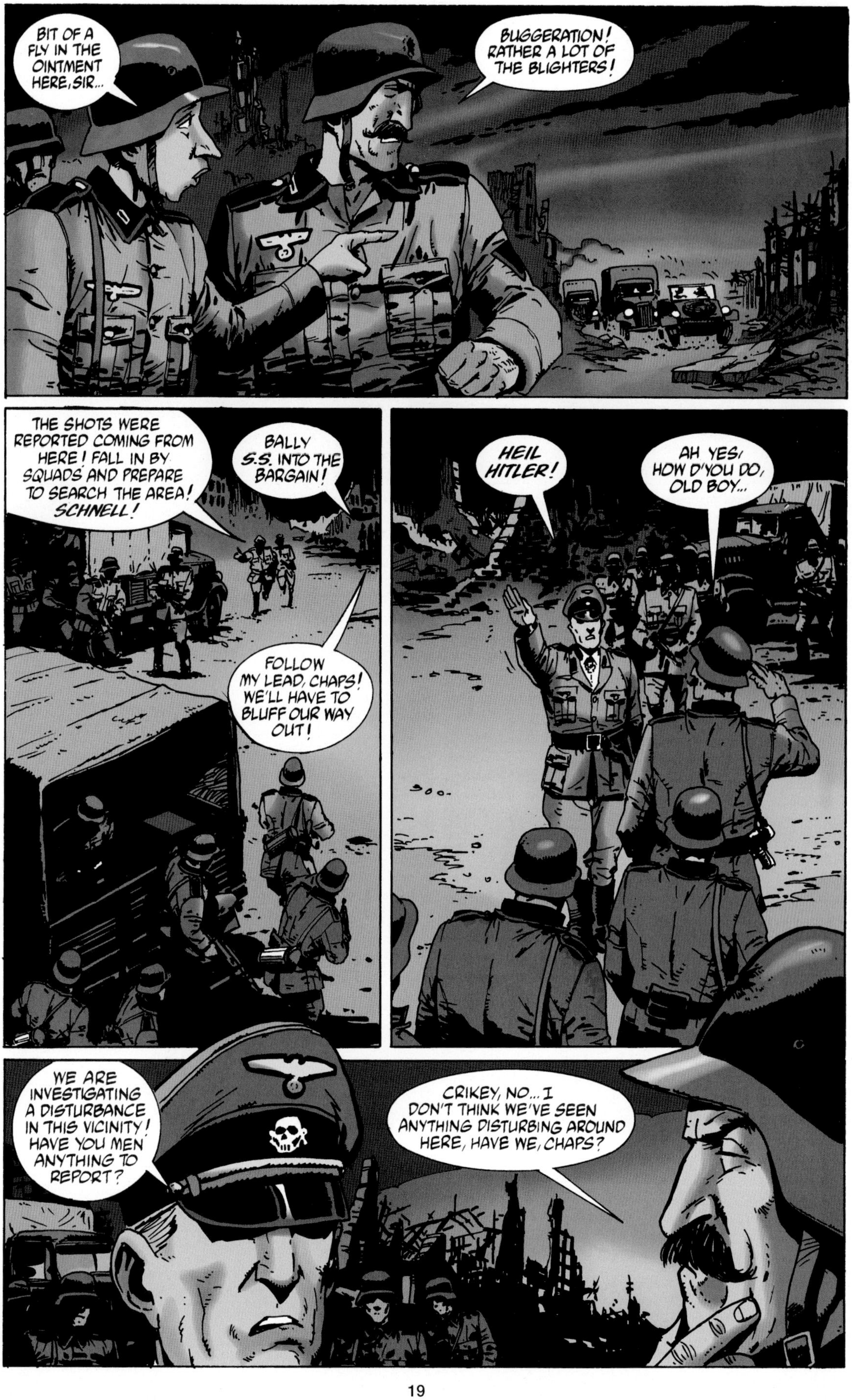

THE SHOTS WERE REPORTED COMING FROM HERE! FALL IN BY SQUADS AND PREPARE TO SEARCH THE AREA! SCHNELL!
BALLY S.S. INTO THE BARGAIN!
FOLLOW MY LEAD, CHAPS! WE'LL HAVE TO BLUFF OUR WAY OUT!
HEIL HITLER!
AH YES, HOW D'YOU DO, OLD BOY...
WE ARE INVESTIGATING A DISTURBANCE IN THIS VICINITY! HAVE YOU MEN ANYTHING TO REPORT?
CRIKEY, NO... I DON'T THINK WE'VE SEEN ANYTHING DISTURBING AROUND HERE, HAVE WE, CHAPS?

VERY WELL! SPREAD OUT AND SEARCH, MEN!
YES, OFF YOU GO... JOLLY NICE TALKING TO YOU... TOODLE-PIP...

GUTEN NACHT, BOYS.
UM..YES, NIGHTY-NIGHT...
WIEDERSEHEN.
MM-HMM, YES. REGARDS TO YOUR SISTER, OLD MAN.

BEST OF LUCK, JA?
ABSOLUTELY, FRITZ. LOT OF WEATHER WE'RE HAVING, MM?
I SAY, SIR, WHAT AN UTTERLY SPLENDID WHEEZE! IT'S WORKING LIKE A CHARM!

JUST REQUIRES A LITTLE BRAVADO, DOUBTFUL, THAT'S ALL.
OLD CHUM OF MINE TRIED IT IN KENYA ONCE. HAD TO GET PAST A TRIBE OF MOUNTAIN GORILLAS FOR SOME REASON, SO HE MADE A DISGUISE OUT OF COCONUT HALVES AND AN OLD ARMY GREATCOAT AND WALKED RIGHT UP TO 'EM, BOLD AS BRASS.
ONLY TROUBLE WAS HE COULDN'T QUITE LOOK 'EM IN THE EYE, AND THE NEXT THING HE KNEW THE BLOODY THINGS WERE TAKING IT IN TURNS TO MATE WITH HIM. NEVER THE SAME AGAIN.

BROWNEYE BRONSON, THAT WAS HIS NAME! MAD AS A LOBSTER...
AND DEAD, SIR.

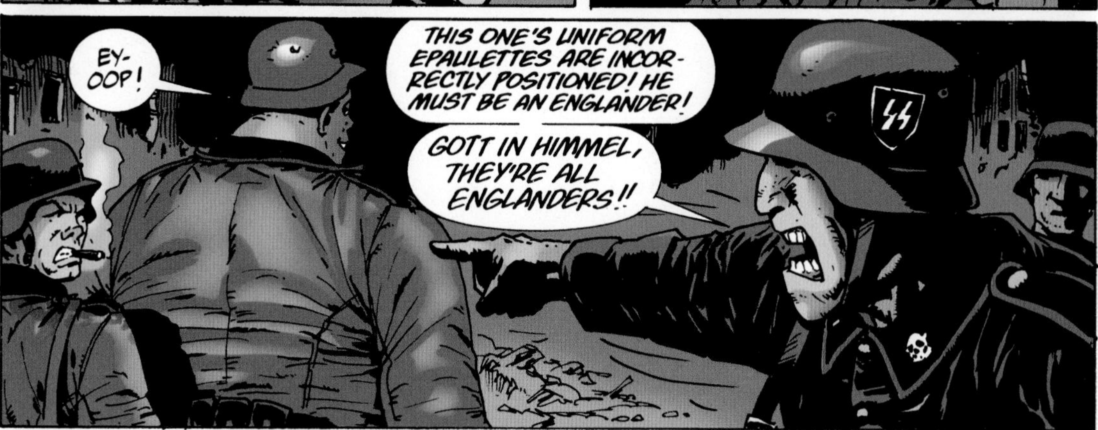

THAT'S TORN IT! TALLY HO!!

HOT LEAD, THAT'S THE STUFF TO GIVE 'EM!
NOT LIKE YOU TO MAKE A SIMPLE MISTAKE LIKE THAT, SAR'NT!
EY-OOP!
I MUST SAY, I ALWAYS FIND THIS PART MOST UNPLEASANT...!

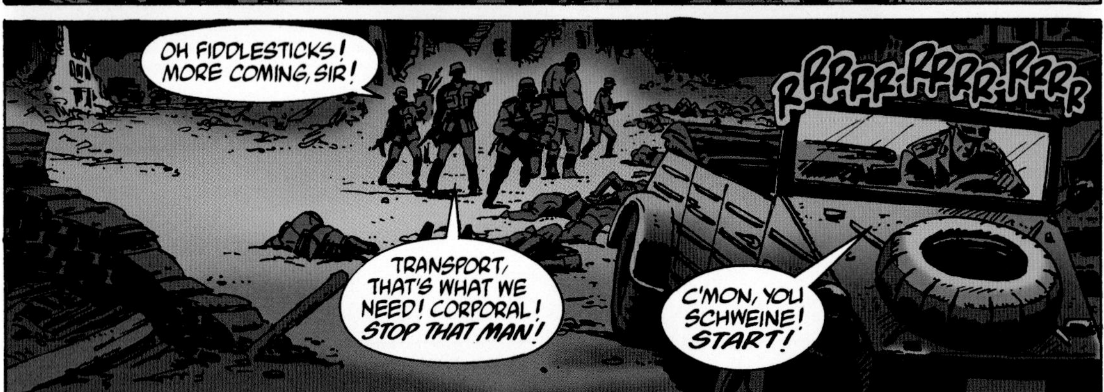
OH FIDDLESTICKS! MORE COMING, SIR!
RRRRR-RRRR-RRRR
TRANSPORT, THAT'S WHAT WE NEED! CORPORAL! STOP THAT MAN!
C'MON, YOU SCHWEINE! START!

YER AHT OF ORDAH!!
CHONK!

NEE-NAR-NEE-NYEE-NYEE-NAH-NAR
FULL STEAM AHEAD, DOUBTFUL!
PIPER--THE BLUE BOLLOCK!

KASINO
SO HOW WOULD YOU GIRLS LIKE A LOOK AT MY *BIG TANK*...?

OH, OBERST FLASCHMANN! COULD WE *REALLY*?
YOU ARE THE REICH'S MOST CELEBRATED PANZER COMMANDER, HERR OBERST! WE WOULD *LOVE* TO SEE YOUR MIGHTY WEAPON!
OTTO, MY DEARS. CALL ME OTTO...

I'LL GIVE YOU SOMETHING TO TO FIDDLE WITH WHILE BERLIN BURNS, MEIN FRAULEINS!
Hee hee!

I'LL BE SHOWING THESE TWO THE *MAIN ARMAMENT* TONIGHT, WILLI-- SO BE SURE AND TAKE THE LONG WAY HOME, *eh*?
RIGHT YOU ARE, HERR OBERST!

AH--DOES ANYONE KNOW WHERE WE'RE ACTUALLY GOING?
ONE MOMENT, DOUBTFUL. I'M TRYING TO FIND THE MAP--

SEE HOW LONG AND SHINY IT IS, LADIES? FOR EXTRA PENETRATION, YOU SEE!
OOOOOH!

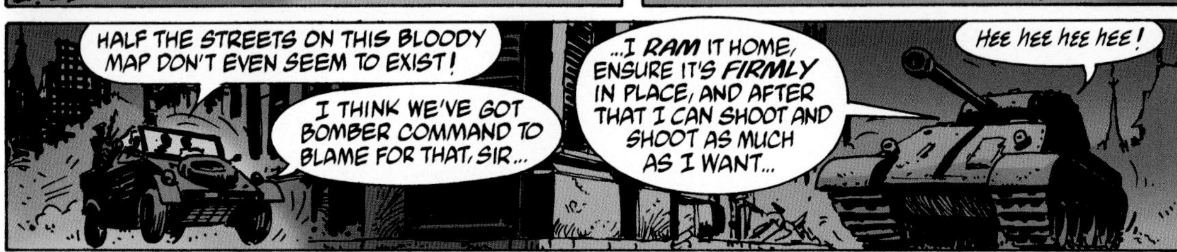
HALF THE STREETS ON THIS BLOODY MAP DON'T EVEN SEEM TO EXIST!
I THINK WE'VE GOT BOMBER COMMAND TO BLAME FOR THAT, SIR...
...I RAM IT HOME, ENSURE IT'S FIRMLY IN PLACE, AND AFTER THAT I CAN SHOOT AND SHOOT AS MUCH AS I WANT...
Hee hee hee hee!

SCHEISSE!
WHOOPS!
BUGGER AND BLAST IT!

WHAT THE HELL WAS THAT?!

BACK THE WAY WE CAME, DOUBTFUL! DON'T SPARE THE HORSES!
ONE MOMENT, ENGLANDERS...!
AH...

I'D ADVISE YOU TO STAY WHERE YOU ARE, MY FRIENDS. I'VE GOT SEVENTY-FIVE MILLIMETERS HERE, AND I KNOW HOW TO USE EVERY INCH OF IT.
412

OH, ARSE.
HOW DID YOU KNOW WE WERE ENGLISH, FRITZ?

YOU WERE DRIVING ON THE LEFT, TOMMY.
FOR YOU THE WAR IS OVER, YES?

POOR SHOW, DOUBTFUL. ABSOLUTE COCK-UP.

AH, YES SIR, QUITE SECOND-ELEVEN. I'M AWFULLY SORRY, I DON'T KNOW WHAT I WAS THINKING...

ACH, NEVER MIND, ENGLANDERS!

THE GESTAPO!!
INDEED! 
THE RATHER... SHORT TIME YOU WILL BE SPENDING AS OUR GUESTS WILL BE ANYTHING BUT COZY, GENTLEMEN. THERE IS NO DOUBT MUCH THAT THE INFAMOUS RIFLE BRIGADE WILL BE ABLE TO TELL US ABOUT BRITISH INTELLIGENCE PLANNING FOR THE SECOND FRONT...
AND-- AS YOU CAN NO DOUBT IMAGINE--
WE HAVE PLENTY OF WAYS OF MAKING YOU TALK...!
NEXT: A TASTE OF BRITISH BEEF

BOLLAND

WELL, WELL, WELL. DARCY, MILK, CRUMB, GEEZER, THE PIPER AND HANK THE YANK...
THE INFAMOUS RIFLE BRIGADE.
GOOD CHRIST!
MUMMY!
EY-OOP!
YER AHT OF ORDAH!
GAWD DAMMIT!
Definitely Not Cricket
Garth Ennis writer
Carlos Ezquerra artist
Patricia Mulvihill colorist
Jamison separator
Clem Robins letters
Brian Bolland cover
Jennifer Lee asst. editor
Axel Alonso editor

I AM **GERTA GASCH,** GENTLEMEN. IT IS MY JOB TO ENSURE YOUR INTERROGATION IS AS UNPLEASANT AS POSSIBLE-- AND MAKE NO MISTAKE ABOUT IT, ***IT WILL BE.***

EVEN IN THE GESTAPO I AM FEARED FOR MY ***RIGOROUS PUMPINGS...***

THIS IS OUTRAGEOUS! I DEMAND THOSE PRISONERS BE TURNED OVER TO ME AT ONCE!

YOU DEMAND, OBERST FLASCHMANN...?
I CAPTURED THOSE ENGLANDERS SINGLE-HANDEDLY! THEY ARE PRISONERS OF THE GERMAN WEHRMACHT, NOT YOU BOOTLICKING GESTAPO THUGS!

OH YES, AND I'M SURE THIS IS ALL FOR THE BENEFIT OF THE WEHRMACHT, ISN'T IT?
"TOP PANZER ACE FOILS BRITISH TERRORISTS"! "HERO OF THE REICH DOES IT AGAIN"! "FLASCHMANN BACK IN TOWN--RUSSIAN FRONT VET GETS THE FRAULEINS WET"!
YOU ARE CHASING HEADLINES AGAIN, OBERST. YOU ARE PATHETIC.

LOOK, WANKSHAFT, OR WHATEVER YOUR NAME IS--
VENKSCHAFT. HAUPTMANN VENKSCHAFT.
I WOULD ADVISE YOU TO CHOOSE YOUR NEXT WORDS WITH ENORMOUS CARE...

DON'T THREATEN ME, YOU TWISTED LITTLE CRUMB OF ARSEMEAT! I WAS HAVING THE SHIT KICKED OUT OF ME AT STALINGRAD WHEN YOU WERE JUNIOR BOLLOCK INSPECTOR AT THE HAMBURG V.D. CLINIC!
HOW DARE YOU! IT WAS VITAL WAR WORK!
I HAVE THE KNIGHTS CROSS WITH OAK LEAVES, PINNED ON ME BY ADOLF HIMSELF! WHAT HAVE YOU GOT, A CERTIFICATE IN PUBE-SHAMPOOING?
SO, YOU INSULT THE FUHRER! YOU MENTION HIS NAME IN THE SAME BREATH AS PUBE-SHAMPOOING!
I HAVE POWERFUL FRIENDS, WANKSHAFT...
VENK... SCHAFT...
WE WILL SEE HOW CLEVER YOU ARE WHEN I REPORT YOUR GROSS EXCESS OF AUTHORITY! I WILL BE BACK FOR MY PRISONERS, HAUPTMANN!
POWERFUL FRIENDS...! IF YOU MEAN THOSE PRUSSIAN OAFS WHO DON'T KNOW YOU'RE SLIPPING THEIR FAT OLD WIVES THE BRATWURST, I CAN ONLY WISH YOU LUCK! SEE HOW FAR YOU GET, OBERST!
FINE!
FINE!

MY SUPERIORS WANT INFORMATION ON YOUR SECOND FRONT, GENTLE-MEN--
--YOUR MUCH-VAUNTED D-DAY. THOUGH WHY WE SHOULD FEAR INVASION IF YOU ARE THE BEST THEY CAN SEND...!
THE MIGHTY RIFLE BRIGADE! THE BRITISH ARMY'S FINEST! PAH! A WORTHLESS COLLEC-TION OF FREAKS AND DEGENERATES!
YOU DECADENT BRITISH ARE WEAK--BUT WE GERMANS ARE STRONG! OUR REICH WILL LAST A THOUSAND YEARS!
YES, YES, SO WE'VE HEARD...
WELL COME ON, SERIOUSLY, WHAT IS THE THING IN THE SKIRT? IS IT EVEN A MAN?
AND LOOK! HERE! AN AMER-IKANER! TYPICAL ENGLANDERS--NOT ENOUGH OF THEIR OWN TO MAKE UP THE NUMBERS, SO THEY RUN CRYING TO UNCLE SAM...
GAWD DAMMIT!
YES, WELL, TYPICAL BLOODY JERRY! MAD AS A TABLE AND TWICE AS STUPID!
THE SIMPLEST SCHOOLBOY KNOWS THAT AMERICA IS A BRITISH COLONY...!

WHAT?
OH YES, WELL-KNOWN FACT. ONE OF OUR MANY SPLENDID IMPERIAL POSSESSIONS IN FAROFF LANDS, LOYALLY SENDING THEIR STOUT-HEARTED, SIMPLE, HONEST SONS TO DEFEND THE MOTHER COUNTRY IN TIME OF NEED.
RATHER LIKE SCOTLAND, SAY, OR THE EAST END OF LONDON...
YER AHT OF ORDAH!
GAWD DAMMIT!

I BALLY WELL OUGHT TO REMEMBER IT, I ORGANIZED IT!
YES, ON MY OLD CHUM BELL-END BRISCO'S TEA PLANTATION, DEEP IN DARKEST GAMBIA...

Ah... BEG PARDON?
I GREW UP IN AFRICA, ON MY FAMILY'S LITTLE MONKEY FARM IN THE M'BOPPO VALLEY. I WAS HAPPY THERE.
UNTIL THE DAY MY FATHER WENT TO THE OUTHOUSE WITH A SET OF PORNOGRAPHIC POST-CARDS HE'D BOUGHT IN CASABLANCA...
TALLY-HOOOOO...!
SHLP SHLP SHLP SHLP

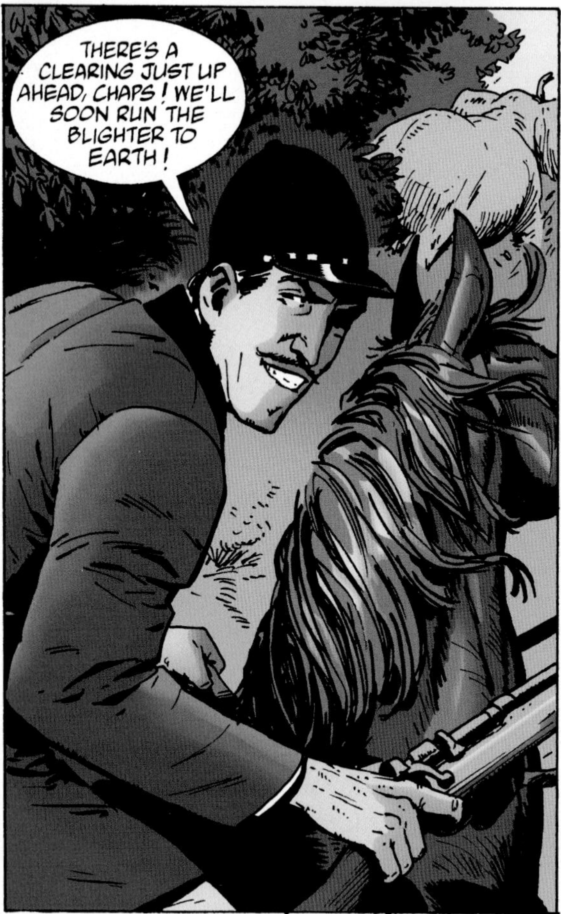
THERE'S A CLEARING JUST UP AHEAD, CHAPS! WE'LL SOON RUN THE BLIGHTER TO EARTH!

SHLP SHLP SHLP SHLP SHLP
ACH! WHAT'S THAT VERDAMMT COMMOTION OUT THERE?

"I WILL NEVER FORGET THE AWFUL SIGHT THAT MET MY EYES, WHEN I CAME RUNNING AT MY FATHER'S SCREAM..."

AND I WILL NEVER FORGET YOUR FACE, CAPTAIN!
OH YES! I WATCHED YOU! RIDING MERRILY ON YOUR WAY, AS IF MY DARLING FATHER'S DEATH MEANT NOTHING TO YOU!
I DIDN'T EVEN SEE HIM! FOR HEAVEN'S SAKE, WOMAN, HE WAS SQUASHED FLAT BY AN ELEPHANT!

YOU EVIL, TWISTED SCHWEINE!
SINCE THAT DAY A TERRIBLE HATE HAS FESTERED IN MY HEART--A HATE FOR YOU, HUGO DARCY! AND WHEN I FOUND YOUR FILE AT GESTAPO HEAD-QUARTERS, WHEN I READ OF YOUR EXPLOITS WITH THIS SQUAD OF IMBECILES, I KNEW THAT ONE DAY MY TIME WOULD COME!

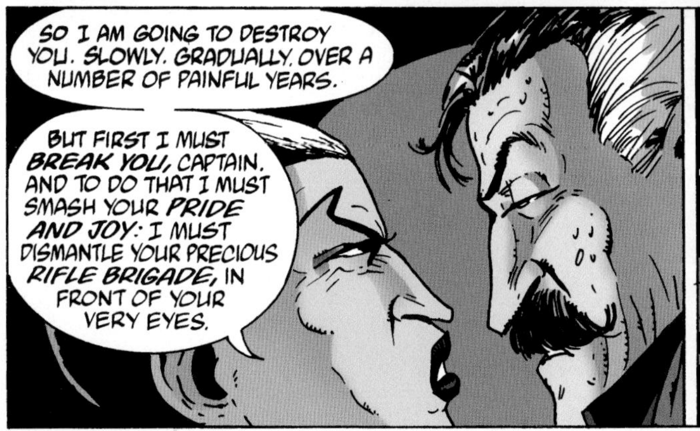
SO I AM GOING TO DESTROY YOU. SLOWLY. GRADUALLY. OVER A NUMBER OF PAINFUL YEARS.
BUT FIRST I MUST BREAK YOU, CAPTAIN. AND TO DO THAT I MUST SMASH YOUR PRIDE AND JOY: I MUST DISMANTLE YOUR PRECIOUS RIFLE BRIGADE, IN FRONT OF YOUR VERY EYES.

BEGINNING WITH ITS WEAKEST LINK...
ULP!

EY-OOP!
KRENK
GOOD SHOW, SAR'NT!
QUICK AS YOU CAN, CHAPS. BEFORE THAT BLOODY HARPY COMES BACK AND--

OH, DASH IT ALL!
NOT THINKING OF LEAVING US, WERE YOU, GENTLE-MEN?
PLEASE, DO NOT BE SO HASTY. I HAVE SOMETHING THAT BELONGS TO YOU.

FLUMP
DOUBTFUL!

YOU FIENDISH NAZI HARRIDAN! LOOK WHAT YOUR BULLY BOYS HAVE DONE!
F-FELT SOMETHING BREAK INSIDE ME, ROUND ABOUT THE FORTY-THIRD KICK IN THE GOOLIES...MUST BE--GAACH-- BLEEDING INTERNALLY...

GOSH, WE'VE...BEEN IN SOME SCRAPES TOGETHER, HAVEN'T WE, SIR? BUT IT LOOKS LIKE MY NUMBER'S UP...
OH GOD, THE HUMANITY! IF ONLY THERE WAS SOME-THING I COULD DO!

THERE IS... ONE THING, ACTUALLY...

ANYTHING, DOUBTFUL! ANYTHING TO--TO MAKE IT EASIER!
ANY... THING...?
YES, YES! YOU'VE GOT MY WORD ON IT, OLD MAN!

THEN GIVE MY JOHN THOMAS A RUB, SIR...
WHAT?!
LIKE NANNY USED TO DO... WHAT IS IT HANK THE YANK'S CHAPS CALL IT... A HAND JOB, YES, THAT'S IT...
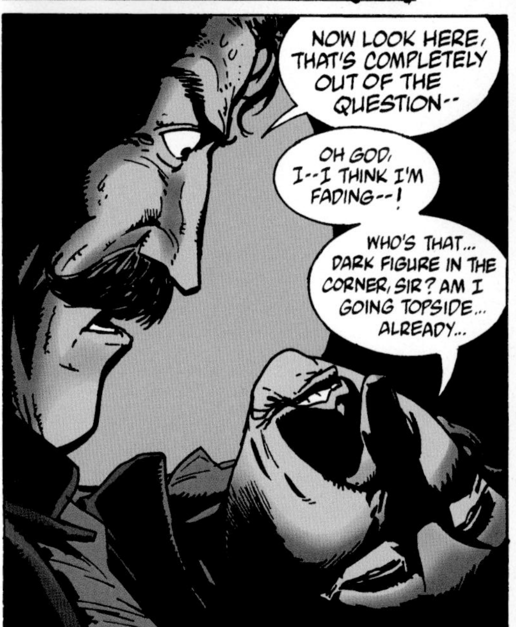
NOW LOOK HERE, THAT'S COMPLETELY OUT OF THE QUESTION--
OH GOD, I--I THINK I'M FADING--!
WHO'S THAT... DARK FIGURE IN THE CORNER, SIR? AM I GOING TOPSIDE... ALREADY...

OH CHRIST.
JUST THINK OF ENGLAND, SIR... I KNOW I WILL...

TELL MY MOTHER I
HACCCH-PTOOOCHH

WHAT THE DICKENS-- THAT'S NOT INTERNAL BLEEDING, THAT'S JUST A COUPLE OF BUSTED TEETH!
GOODNESS ME, SO IT IS! WELL, ISN'T THAT A RELIEF, I'M GOING TO MAKE IT AFTER ALL!

BUT... BUT...
HMMM.
OH, WELL DON'T LET US INTERRUPT YOU!

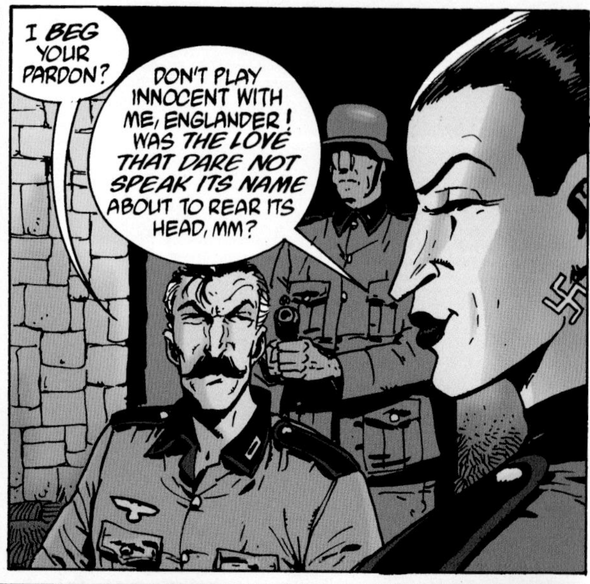
I BEG YOUR PARDON?
DON'T PLAY INNOCENT WITH ME, ENGLANDER! WAS THE LOVE THAT DARE NOT SPEAK ITS NAME ABOUT TO REAR ITS HEAD, MM?

HOW DARE YOU? WHY, IF YOU WEREN'T ONE OF THE WEAKER SEX, I'D--
YES, I CAN IMAGINE! I KNOW YOUR DIRTY LITTLE SECRET!

UNHAND ME, MADAM-- GUMF
WHAT'S THE MATTER, CAPTAIN? DOES MY WOMANLY BODY INTIMIDATE YOU?
HA! I KNOW WHAT ENGLISHMEN ARE HIDING BEHIND THEIR STIFF UPPER LIPS!

CEASE THIS FOOLISH PRETENSE! YOU FORGET THAT I HAVE READ YOUR FILES! I KNOW YOU HAVE INDULGED BEFORE!
YES, CAPTAIN DARCY! I KNOW YOU WENT TO PUBLIC SCHOOL!

OH, IT DOESN'T COUNT IF IT'S AT SCHOOL, FOR CRYING OUT LOUD! EVERYONE KNOWS THAT!
IT PREVENTS ALL SORTS OF TURKISHNESS LATER ON IN A CHAP'S LIFE, NOT TO MENTION ITS EFFECT ON CHARACTER AND SELF-DISCIPLINE. JUST ONE OF THE MANY BENEFITS OF AN ENGLISH PUBLIC SCHOOL EDUCATION...

THEY DO SAY THE BATTLE OF WATERLOO WAS WON IN THE DORM AFTER LIGHTS OUT AT ETON...
YOUR VILE SLURS ARE ENTIRELY WITHOUT SUBSTANCE, FRAULEIN GASCH!
THAT SORT OF THING MIGHT BE ALL VERY WELL FOR YOUR GREEKS AND ROMANS-- OH YES, BY THUNDER! I'VE SEEN WHAT HAPPENS ON THE SIDES OF THOSE VASES!

BUT NOT FOR ENGLISHMEN!
WHY, THE IDEA THAT ONE CHAP COULD LOVE ANOTHER-- PAH! ABSOLUTE TWADDLE!

YES, WELL, WE'LL LEAVE THE PSYCHOLOGICAL TORMENT ASIDE FOR THE MOMENT. LET'S SEE HOW YOU RESPOND TO THE SAVAGE BEATING INSTEAD...
DO YOUR WORST, YOU LOATHSOME DRAB! YOU WON'T BREAK "KHYBER" DARCY!

I DO SO LIKE A CHALLENGE...

GENTLE-MEN! I GIVE YOU "KHYBER" DARCY...

POST MY WORST.
UHHHH...
NO!!

YOU ABSOLUTE ROTTERS! WHAT HAVE YOU DONE TO HIM?
I HAVE SIMPLY TAUGHT HIM THE FOLLY OF DEFYING THE IRON WILL OF THE GERMAN REICH.
HAVEN'T I, CAPTAIN? COME ON! SAY IT LIKE I TOLD YOU!

SAY IT! SAY "HITLER IS MY ONE TRUE AND RIGHTFUL FUHRER!"
SAY IT, SCHWEINE!

HH... HHHH...
I HAVE BROKEN YOU! IT IS USELESS TO RESIST! COME ON, SAY IT!
HITLER...
YES! YES!!

HAS ONLY GOT ONE ♪ BALL...!

WHAT?!
THE OTHER! IS IN THE AL-BERT HALL! ♪

I KNEW THEY'D NEVER BREAK HIM!
HIMMLER! HAS ♫ SOMETHING SIM'LAR!
COME ON, CHAPS! SING WITH YOUR CAPTAIN!

BUT POOR OLD GOEBBELS, HAS NO BALLS, AT ALL! ♪
CEASE THIS BLASPHEMY! NEIN! NEIN! NEIIINNN!

HITLER! HAS ONLY GOT ONE BALL!
WHAT THE HELL IS GOING ON?
THE ENGLANDERS, HERR HAUPTMANN! THEIR DEFIANT SINGING IS INSPIRING THE OTHER PRISONERS TO RESIST!

THE OTHER! IS IN THE AL-BERT HALL!

HIMMLER! HAS SOMETHING SIM'LAR!

BUT POOR OLD GOEBBELS, HAS NO BALLS, AT ALL!
AAGH!

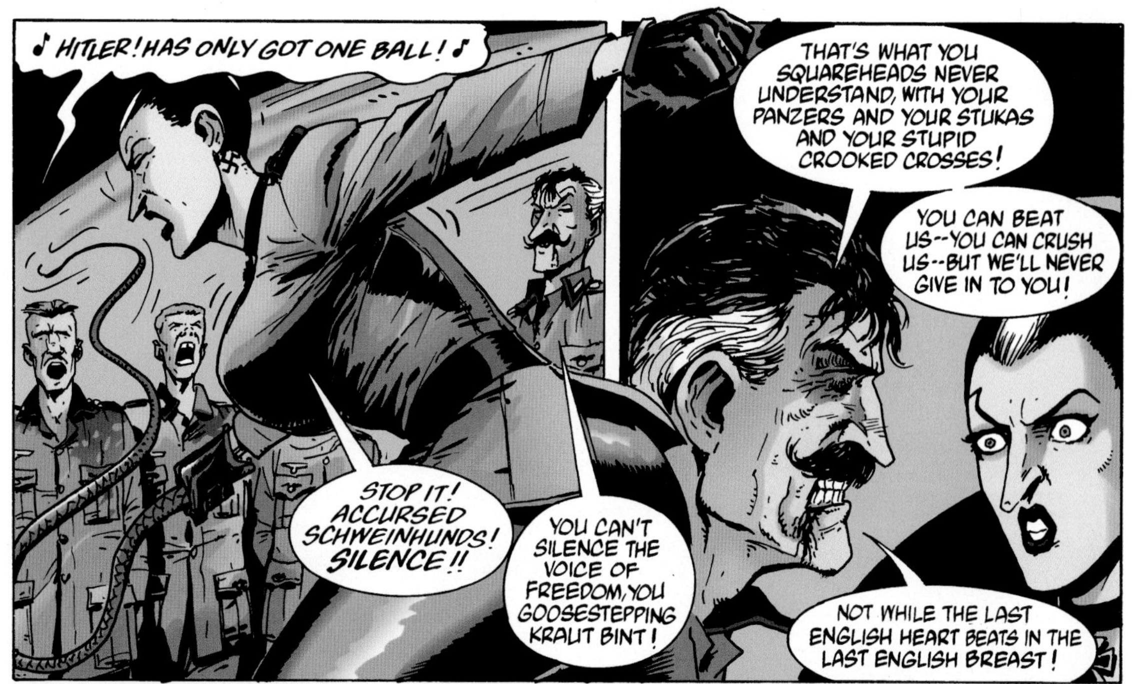

THERE'LL ALWAYS BE AN ENGLAND, FRITZ! I WOULDN'T GIVE YOUR BLOODY SILLY THIRD REICH *SIX MONTHS*, LET ALONE A THOUSAND YEARS!

THERE'LL ALWAYS BE AN ENGLAND--AND SO LONG AS THERE'S A *DARCY* TO LEAD 'EM, THERE'LL ALWAYS BE A *RIFLE BRIGADE*!

WHY, THERE WAS A RIFLE BRIGADE BEFORE THERE WERE RIFLES! BECAUSE SOONER OR LATER, A JOB COMES ALONG THAT ORDINARY CHAPS CAN'T DO!
A JOB FOR THE SPECIAL SPECIAL FORCES! BY THE LORD HARRY, YES! WHEN THE MARINES HAVE GOT A HEAD-ACHE--WHEN THE PARAS SCREAM LIKE SCHOOLGIRLS--WHEN THE S.A.S. FOUL THEIR BRITCHES--
YOU SEND FOR THE RIFLE BRIGADE!
♪ BUT POOR OLD GOEBBELS, HAS NO BALLS, AT ALL!
SO THERE!
MUTTER HILFE, IT JUST ISN'T FAIR...!

I MUST SAY, SIR, SPLENDID SHOW OF BRITISH PLUCK BACK THERE. ABSOLUTELY FIRST-RATE.
GOT TO REMIND THE HUN WHO'S BOSS, DOUBTFUL. EVEN IF THEY ARE GOING TO BUNG US IN FRONT OF A FIRING SQUAD AT FIRST LIGHT.

THE LAST HURRAH OF THE RIFLE BRIGADE, *eh*?
HMMM...UNDER THE CIRCS, IT WOULDN'T HURT FOR US TO HEAR WHAT OUR MISSION WAS GOING TO BE, WOULD IT?
YES, WON'T MAKE MUCH DIFFERENCE NOW...
NEED-TO-KNOW BASIS BE DAMNED, DOUBTFUL. OFF YOU GO.

BEG PARDON, SIR?
OFF YOU GO. THE MISSION, DOUBTFUL. TELL US ABOUT THE OP.

BUT YOU'RE THE C.O., YOU'RE THE ONE WITH THE GEN...
NORMALLY I WOULD BE, BUT I ASSUMED YOU WERE CARRYING SEALED ORDERS FROM COLONEL FRIGPIPE AT INTELLIGENCE. YOU'D HAND THEM OVER TO ME WHEN WE NEARED OUR OBJECTIVE.
WE'VE DONE IT THAT WAY BEFORE...

AH... YEEEES...
BUT WHY WOULD YOU THINK WE WERE DOING IT THIS TIME?
STOP PLAYING SILLY BUGGERS, WILL YOU, DOUBTFUL...?

YOU KNOW PERFECTLY WELL YOU WERE THE ONE WHO TELEPHONED ME. "IT'S ON TONIGHT," YOU SAID.
SO I DID WHAT I ALWAYS DO WHEN WE'RE LAYING ON ONE OF THESE SHOWS: GATHERED THE CHAPS, SCROUNGED UP THE STENS AND THE STICKY BOMBS, HITCHED US A LIFT ON A LANC BOUND SAUSAGE-SIDE, AND IT'S OFF WE JOLLY WELL GO...

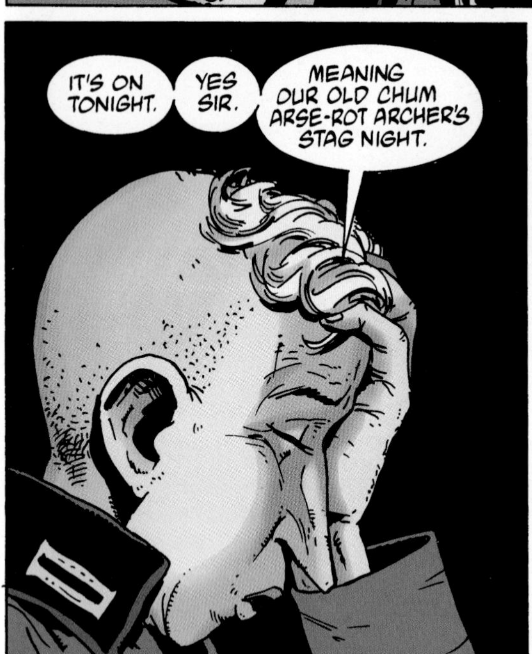
IT'S ON TONIGHT.
YES SIR.
MEANING OUR OLD CHUM ARSE-ROT ARCHER'S STAG NIGHT.

AH.

I SAY... SO WHEN I 'PHONED BACK TO TELL YOU IT WAS ALL ARRANGED AND THE BERLIN EXPRESS LEFT AT SEVEN, YOU ASSUMED AN OP HAD COME UP AND WE'D HAVE TO SKIP THE PARTY...
WHICH... MEANS...
YES SIR.
WE'VE GONE ON A COMMANDO RAID BY MISTAKE.

EY-OOP--!
GAWD DAMMIT!
YER AHT OF ORDAH!
QUIET IN THE RANKS, YOU MEN!
I SAY, WHAT A BIND...!

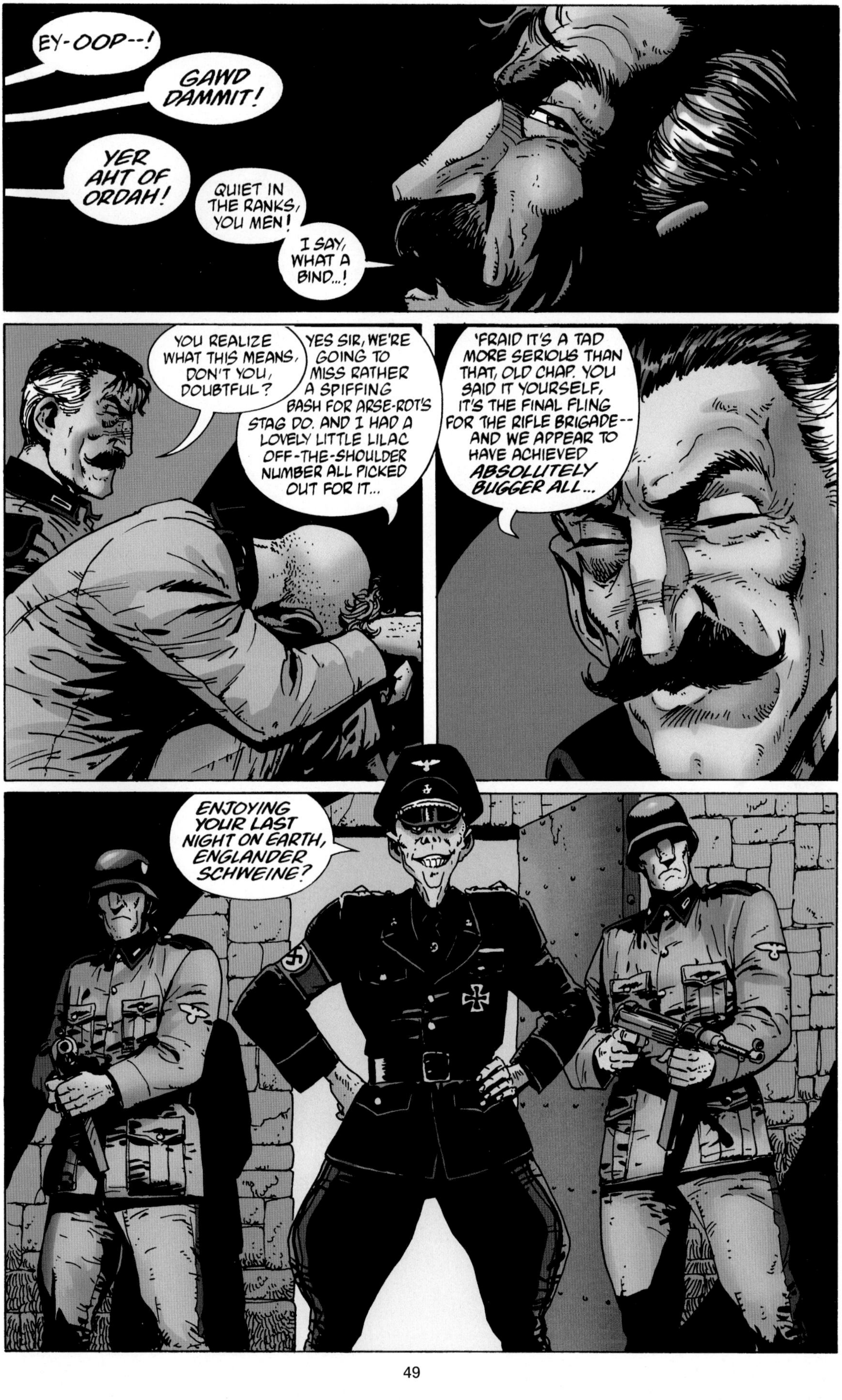

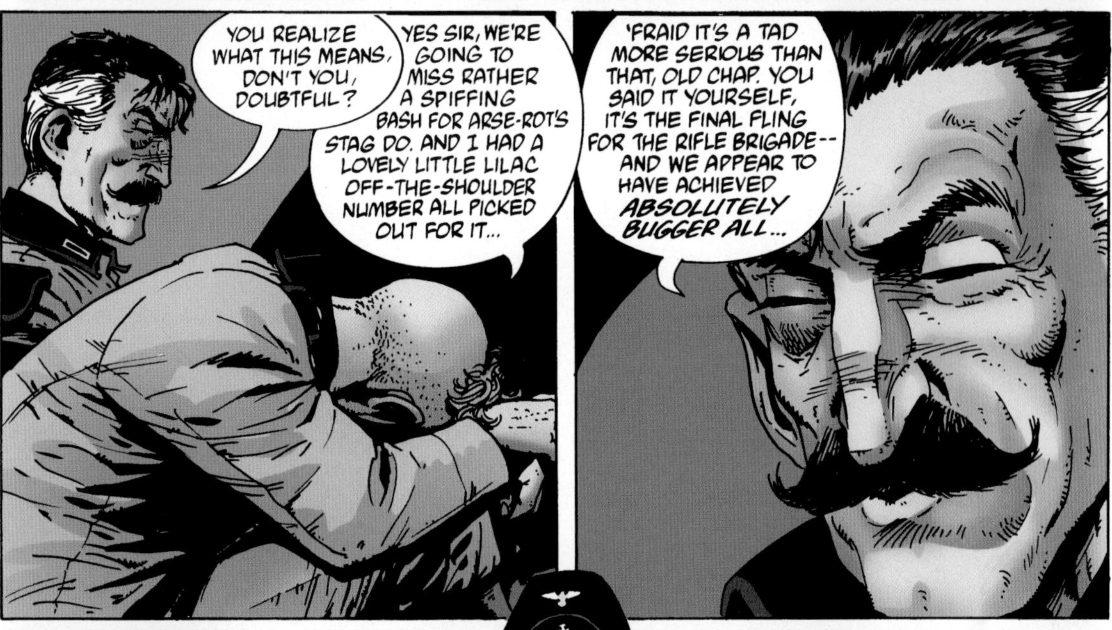
YOU REALIZE WHAT THIS MEANS, DON'T YOU, DOUBTFUL?
YES SIR, WE'RE GOING TO MISS RATHER A SPIFFING BASH FOR ARSE-ROT'S STAG DO. AND I HAD A LOVELY LITTLE LILAC OFF-THE-SHOULDER NUMBER ALL PICKED OUT FOR IT...
'FRAID IT'S A TAD MORE SERIOUS THAN THAT, OLD CHAP. YOU SAID IT YOURSELF, IT'S THE FINAL FLING FOR THE RIFLE BRIGADE--AND WE APPEAR TO HAVE ACHIEVED *ABSOLUTELY BUGGER ALL*...

ENJOYING YOUR LAST NIGHT ON EARTH, ENGLANDER SCHWEINE?

PAH! YOUR FAMOUS BRITISH WIT IS WASTED ON ME, GENTLEMEN!

YOU MAY HAVE GIVEN FRAULEIN GASCH A NERVOUS BREAKDOWN, BUT YOU'LL FIND THAT KURT VENKSCHAFT IS MADE OF STERNER STUFF...
DO BUGGER OFF, FRITZ.
YES, HOW'S A CHAP SUPPOSED TO ENJOY HIS LAST NIGHT ON EARTH WITH YOU WITTERING ON?

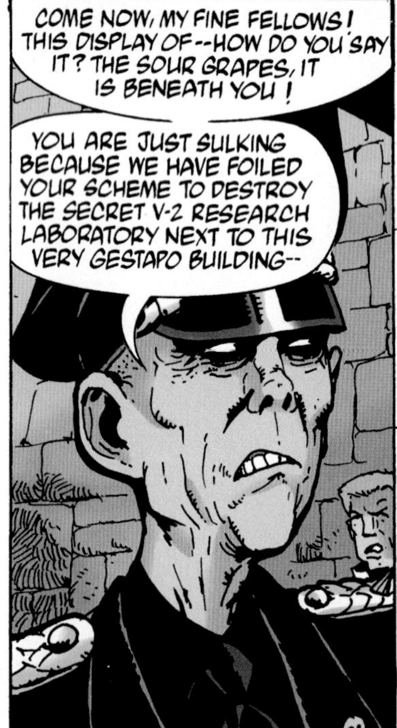

COME NOW, MY FINE FELLOWS! THIS DISPLAY OF--HOW DO YOU SAY IT? THE SOUR GRAPES, IT IS BENEATH YOU!
YOU ARE JUST SULKING BECAUSE WE HAVE FOILED YOUR SCHEME TO DESTROY THE SECRET V-2 RESEARCH LABORATORY NEXT TO THIS VERY GESTAPO BUILDING--

THE ONE SYNTHESIZING FUEL FOR THE ROCKETS THAT WILL SMASH YOUR PATHETIC D-DAY INVASION ON THE BEACHES OF FRANCE!

GO ON...
NEXT: INTO THE BLUE

UP YOURS, FRITZ

GENTLE-
MEN!
REMEMBER YOUR OLD PAL
OBERST FLASCHMANN...?

AH YES. NOW LOOK HERE, I'VE A NUMBER OF COMPLAINTS TO MAKE:
SINCE WE ARRIVED HERE, MY CHAPS AND I HAVE HAD TO PUT UP WITH ALL SORTS OF TEDIOUS STRUTTING AND CROWING, BOTH FROM THIS FELLOW WANKSHAFT--
FOR CHRIST'S SAKE! VENKSCHAFT!

...AND ALSO SOME DREADFUL NAZI SLATTERN WHO'D QUITE OBVIOUSLY GONE DOOLALLY.
FURTHERMORE, SECOND-LIEUTENANT MILK AND I HAVE BEEN THOROUGHLY DUFFED UP--A NUMBER OF BLOWS BELOW THE BELT, I'M SORRY TO SAY--AND WORSE STILL, THE SUGGESTION WAS MADE THAT WE'RE BOTH A COUPLE OF WOOPSIES! IT SIMPLY WON'T DO!
OF COURSE NOT, CAPTAIN, OF COURSE NOT! SUCH BARBARITY IS A THING OF THE PAST, BELIEVE ME!

NO, ALL THAT IS REQUIRED NOW IS A PHOTOGRAPH OR TWO, A CHAT WITH THE PROPAGANDA PEOPLE, AND THEN YOU MAY BE ON YOUR WAY TO THE STALAG! YOU SCRATCH MY BACK AND I SCRATCH YOURS, YES?

SO LET'S HAVE PLENTY OF DEJECTED LOOKS FOR THE CAMERAS, eh? EYES FIXED ON BOOTS...BEWILDERED MUMBLING ABOUT THE SHOCK OF BEING CAPTURED SINGLE-HANDEDLY BY THE HEROIC FLASCHMANN...
AND YOU, BIG FELLOW! THAT CHEERY SMILE HAS GOT TO GO!
EY-OOP!

THIS WAY, YOU GET WHAT YOU WANT -- A HAPPY SPELL IN CAPTIVITY, RED CROSS PARCELS, LOTS OF YOUR ENGLISH KNEES UP MOTHER BROWN--
AND I GET WHAT I WANT, WHICH IS PLENTY OF COLUMN INCHES AND A BIG HEADSHOT IN SIGNAL! A REAL LEG-OPENER FOR THE GIRLS AT THE UNTER DEN LINDEN, BELIEVE ME!
WELL, THIS IS, ah... VERY GENEROUS OF YOU, COLONEL...
ACH! THAT'S JUST TO SHOW YOU NOT ALL GERMANS ARE LIKE THESE GESTAPO SWINE!
BLAM
THAT'S JUST IN CASE, FRITZ!
COME ON THE RIFLE BRIGADE!
GAWD DAMMIT!
YER AHT OF ORDAH!
EY-OOP!
LOOKS LIKE THE JACKBOOT'S ON THE OTHER FOOT, YOU TOAD!
OH GOD!

LISTEN CLOSELY, MEN!
WE'RE GOING TO DISPATCH THE REST OF THE GUARDS AND TAKE THEIR WEAPONS! THEN WE'RE GOING TO GAIN ENTRY TO THIS SECRET ROCKET FUEL PLANT NEXT DOOR-
ON CAPTAIN WANKSHAFT'S PERSONAL AUTHORITY--AND BLOW THE WHOLE BALLY THING TO BLAZES!
OH, TOP HOLE, SIR!
WHAT'S THE MATTER WITH HIM...?

I BELIEVE HE WANTS HIS PIPES BACK, CAPTAIN. AND CONSIDERING WHAT HAPPENED TO THE LAST CHAP WHO TOOK THE PIPER'S PIPES, YOU'D BE WELL ADVISED TO GO AND FETCH THEM POST HASTE...
WH-WH-WHAT HAPPENED?

OH JESUS!

AND--
ALL THE ORDNANCE YOU CAN CARRY, FELLOWS!
STOP STARING AT ME, YOU INSANE LITTLE MAN! I'VE GOT YOUR PRECIOUS--

PIPES...

AND--

ARE THESE MEN WITH *YOU*, HERR HAUPTMANN?

MEIN GOTT! THEY'RE ENGLANDERS!

PIPER-- HIGHLAND DONG!

BUDDA BUDDA BUDDA BUDDA

NAAAR-NO-NI-NARR-NI-NI-NEE NAAARR

AAAIIEEE!

AARRGHH!

NEEIIIINNN!

WAAAAAH-NIII-NO BUDDA BUDDA BUDDA BUDDA

AAAAHH!

YYIIIEEHH!

ALL RIGHT, PRIVATE THE YANK, YOU'RE THE EXPLOSIVES EXPERT-- CHUCK A GRENADE IN THAT FUEL VAT AND LET'S BEETLE OFF BACK TO BLIGHTY!

TEUFEL! WHAT HAPPENED HERE?
IT-- HAACH! -- IT WAS ENGLANDER COMMANDOS--
IT WAS THE RIFLE BRIGADE!

I AM HAUPTMANN VENKSCHAFT OF THE GESTAPO!
SINGLE-HANDEDLY I ATTEMPTED TO STOP THE ENGLANDERS FROM DESTROYING THE ROCKET FUEL PLANT--BUT THEY WERE TOO MUCH EVEN FOR ME!
GOTT IN HIMMEL, THE INFAMOUS RIFLE BRIGADE! I MUST INFORM THE FUHRER AT ONCE!

WAIT, WAIT, YOU DON'T UNDERSTAND! THE V-2 FUEL WAS SO SECRET THAT WE ONLY HAD ONE COPY OF THE FORMULA! WE COULDN'T RISK IT GETTING INTO THE WRONG HANDS!
AND NOT ONLY DID THE ENGLANDERS DESTROY EVERY DROP OF FUEL WE HAD, THEY TOOK THE FORMULA WITH THEM!

WE'LL HAVE TO START FROM SCRATCH, IT'LL TAKE US BLOODY MONTHS...
WE'VE ESTABLISHED CONTACT WITH THE FUHRER, SIR!
GIVE IT HERE. I WILL SPEAK TO OUR GLORIOUS LEADER MYSELF.

VENKSCHAFT HERE, MEIN FUHRER--
WANKSHAFT?

VENKSCHAFT!
VENKSCHAFT!
MY NAME IS FUCKING VENKSCHAFT, YOU MAD LITTLE ONE-BOLLOCKED TWAT!

I MEAN--

... JA, MEIN FUHRER, I UNDERSTAND... POSTED TO A PENAL BATTALION ON THE EASTERN FRONT WITH THE RANK OF COCKSUCKER THIRD CLASS, JA... AND THE ENGLANDERS?
WHAT?

A-A-ALERT JAGER X--?!

AND, SOMEWHERE UNPLEASANT--
GGGRRRRRRRRR

BERLIN AIRPORT, SIR!
JUST THE TICKET! MAKE FOR THAT HEINKEL, DOUBTFUL!

WON'T THEY HAVE THE FOCKE-WULFS AFTER US STRAIGHT-AWAY, SIR?
THEY DAREN'T SHOOT US DOWN SO LONG AS WE HAVE THE FORMULA-- BUT JUST IN CASE, LET'S SEE IF WE CAN RUSTLE UP SOME HELP!

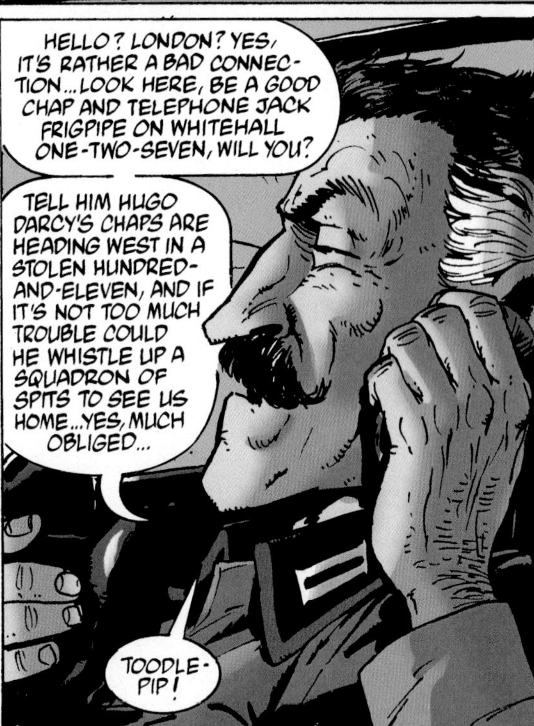
HELLO? LONDON? YES, IT'S RATHER A BAD CONNECTION... LOOK HERE, BE A GOOD CHAP AND TELEPHONE JACK FRIGPIPE ON WHITEHALL ONE-TWO-SEVEN, WILL YOU?
TELL HIM HUGO DARCY'S CHAPS ARE HEADING WEST IN A STOLEN HUNDRED-AND-ELEVEN, AND IF IT'S NOT TOO MUCH TROUBLE COULD HE WHISTLE UP A SQUADRON OF SPITS TO SEE US HOME...YES, MUCH OBLIGED...
TOODLE-PIP!

SHOULDN'T THAT BE IN CODE, SIR?
CODES ARE FOR *GIRLS*, LIEUTENANT.
INFORM THE FUHRER!

WHAT'S THAT JUNKERS UP TO...?
WHO'S THAT JUMPING OUT THE BACK--I SAY, ARE THEY USING PARATROOPS?
GAWD DAMMIT!
YER AHT OF ORDAH!
TH-TH-THAT'S NOT PARATROOPS--!
HUUURRRGG...!
GOOD GOD ALMIGHTY! JAGER X!!

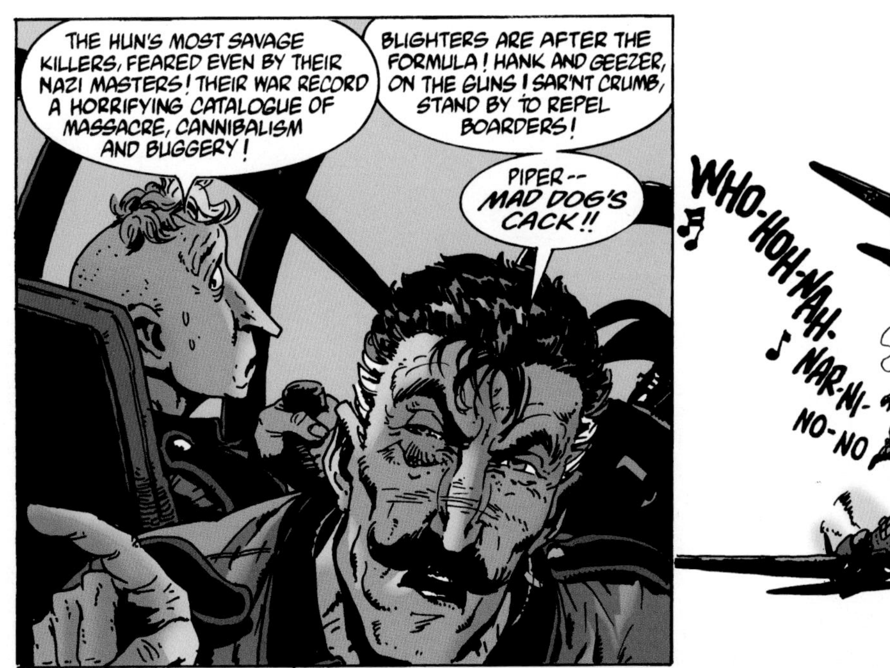
THE HUN'S MOST SAVAGE KILLERS, FEARED EVEN BY THEIR NAZI MASTERS! THEIR WAR RECORD A HORRIFYING CATALOGUE OF MASSACRE, CANNIBALISM AND BUGGERY!
BLIGHTERS ARE AFTER THE FORMULA! HANK AND GEEZER, ON THE GUNS! SAR'NT CRUMB, STAND BY TO REPEL BOARDERS!
PIPER-- MAD DOG'S CACK!!

WHO-HOH-HAH-
NAR-NI-NO-NO
HERE THEY COME!

WATCH THAT SWINE ON THE RIGHT, SIR! I'LL SETTLE HIS JERRY HASH!

AAAIIIEEE!
HOWZAT!

ASTONISHING TACTIC, LIEUTENANT. YOU WILL BE MORE CAREFUL WITH OUR OTHER ENGINE, WON'T YOU?

I--I REALLY AM FRIGHTFULLY SORRY, SIR--!
THAT BIG BUGGER'S AFTER THE OTHER ONE!
GET OUT THERE, SAR'NT!
EY-OOP!
HURRRG...?
HURRRR!
EY-OOP!
SAR'NT CRUMB--!

HE GOT CRUMB, HE-- AAIIIEEE!!
HSSSSHHH! HSSSSHHH!
STEADY, DOUBTFUL!

HSSSSHH--
NOT TODAY, THANK YOU...

I WANT TO GO HOOOMME...!
STOP THAT BLUBBERING AT ONCE! GET HOLD OF YOURSELF, MAN!
NUHHHH!

REALLY, LIEUTENANT! AN ENGLISHMAN DOES NOT CRY ON THE FIELD OF BATTLE!
HE MIGHT GO AWAY AND WRITE A BIT OF POETRY ABOUT IT AFTER-WARDS, BUT OTHERWISE HE CONDUCTS HIMSELF WITH DIGNITY AT ALL TIMES!
NUHHHHH!

YER AHT OF ORDAH!
KLOMP!
GOOD SHOW, CORPORAL...

NEE-NO-NI-NAR-NAR-
AAARRRGGGHH--
-NI-NI-NO-NAR-NI-
RRRTCHH
FIRST-CLASS WORK, PIPER! ONE TO GO!
WE'RE LOSING THE PORT ENGINE!
GAWD DAMMIT!
KLANG

FOOM!

GAWD DAMMIT!!
HURR HURR HURR HURR...!

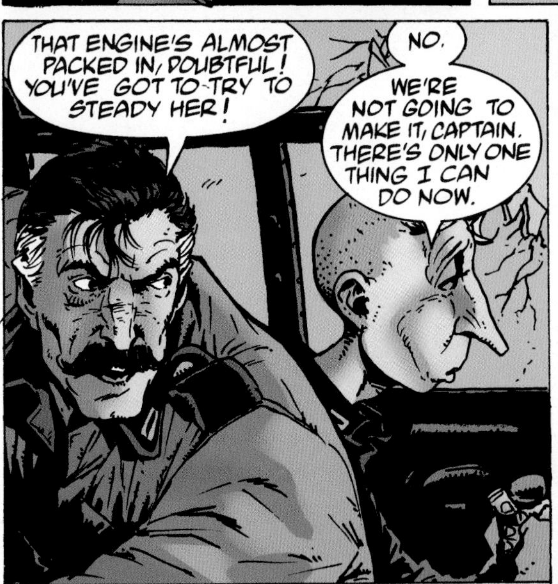
THAT ENGINE'S ALMOST PACKED IN, DOUBTFUL! YOU'VE GOT TO TRY TO STEADY HER!
NO.
WE'RE NOT GOING TO MAKE IT, CAPTAIN. THERE'S ONLY ONE THING I CAN DO NOW.

AND THAT'S TO SAY I LOVE YOU, HUGO DARCY.

...
PARDON?
YOU DON'T KNOW HOW I'VE YEARNED TO SAY THOSE WORDS, SIR! THROUGH ALL THOSE YEARS, ON ALL OUR MISSIONS TOGETHER--NEVER HOPING, NEVER DARING TO DREAM!
BUT I CAN'T HIDE MY FEELINGS ANY LONGER! I CAN'T GO ON LIVING A LIE!

I LOVE YOU, CAPTAIN DARCY! I WANTED TO SPEND THE REST OF MY LIFE WITH YOU! TO BE YOUR BRIDE! TO BEAR YOUR CHILDREN! BUT ALAS, IT CANNOT BE!
KISS ME, MY CAPTAIN! KISS ME A KISS TO BRING OBLIVION!
GET OFF ME, DOUBTFUL! AAAGGHH!
GET OFF AND FLY THE BLOODY PLANE!

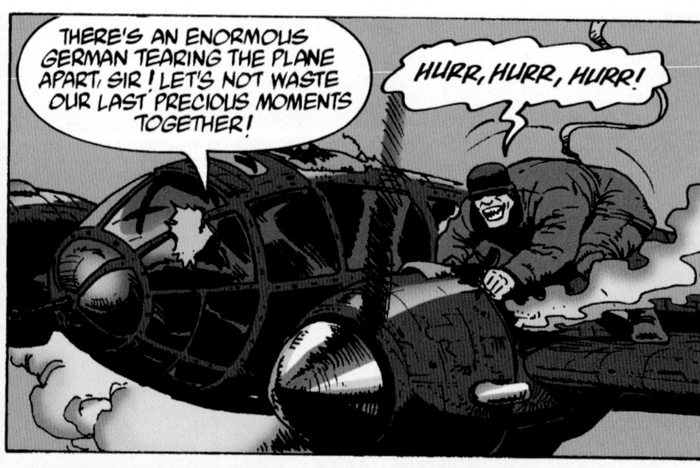
THERE'S AN ENORMOUS GERMAN TEARING THE PLANE APART, SIR! LET'S NOT WASTE OUR LAST PRECIOUS MOMENTS TOGETHER!
HURR, HURR, HURR!

FAB

HURRG...?
EY-OOP!

CHOMP!

AAAIIEE

THAT'S THE WAY, SAR'NT! BITE! BITE HARDER! BITE FOR ENGLAND!
THINK OF THE EMPIRE, SERGEANT CRUMB, AND BITE 'TIL TEETH MEET TEETH!!

RRIIPPP

AAAIIIEEEE

ABSOLUTELY FIRST CLASS! I RATHER THINK THAT MERITS A MENTION IN *DESPATCHES*, DON'T YOU?
B-B-BANDITS TWELVE O'CLOCK HIGH!

OF ALL THE BLASTED LUCK! OUT OF THE FRYING PAN, INTO THE FIRE!

LOOKS LIKE THIS IS IT, YOU CHAPS! IT'S BEEN ABSOLUTELY RIPPING FUN, BUT ALL WE CAN DO NOW IS SHAKE HANDS-- GO DOWN FIGHTING--AND SHOUT HURRAH!
HURRAH FOR THE--

RIFLE BRIGADE...!

FRIGPIPE MUST'VE GOT THE MESSAGE!
GAD! DON'T THEY MAKE YOU FEEL PROUD TO BE BRITISH!
YOU MEAN WE'RE GOING TO MAKE IT AFTER ALL, SIR?

NOW, AH... DOUBTFUL...
I UNDERSTAND YOU'VE BEEN THROUGH RATHER A LOT, AND, um...THE OLD BRAINBOX MIGHT NOT BE FIRING ON ALL CYLINDERS, BUT...BUT I HAVE TO SAY I TAKE A VERY DIM VIEW OF THIS SORT OF...OF THING...
WHAT SORT OF THING IS THAT, SIR?

EH?
YOU KNOW, ALL THAT BALDERDASH YOU WERE SPOUTING A MOMENT AGO, ABOUT-- ABOUT--
ER...
OH, DID I SAY SOMETHING, SIR? I REALLY DON'T REMEMBER; ALL I CAN RECALL DOING IS TRYING TO CONTROL THE PLANE...

BUT-- BUT LOOK HERE, I MEAN TO SAY--
HMMM.

EY-OOP!

BY THE LORD HARRY! WE CLOBBERED THAT ROCKET LAB JUST IN TIME, CHAPS!

D-DAY!!

OH GOSH, SIR, LOOK AT THEM! THE GREATEST ARMADA THE WORLD HAS EVER SEEN! ALL OF OUR PLUCKY CHAPS TOGETHER, SWORN TO DELIVER THE DOWNTRODDEN MASSES OF EUROPE FROM UNDER THE NAZI JACKBOOT!
I SAY, DOUBTFUL, I'VE JUST HAD THE MOST SPLENDID WHEEZE!

HELLO THE FLEET! HUGO DARCY HERE, COMMANDING THE RIFLE BRIGADE!
I WANT YOU FELLOWS TO KEEP BROADCASTING ON ALL CHANNELS--SING YOUR BALLY HEARTS OUT--AND TOGETHER WE'LL SEND FRITZ A MESSAGE HE'LL NEVER FORGET!
READY NOW...!

AYE! GI'E IT THE HAMPDEN ROAR!!

HITLER! HAS ONLY GOT ONE ♪BALL!

THE OTHER! IS IN♪ THE ALBERT HALL!

PS 24
HIMMLER! HAS SOMETHING SIM'LAR!♫

♫BUT POOR OLD GOEBBELS HAS♪ NO BALLS AT ALL!!
ONE MORE TIME, CHAPS!

SHLP SHLP SHLP SHLP
MEIN FUHRER!

F-FORGIVE THIS INTRUSION, MEIN FUHRER, BUT A MASSIVE INVASION FLEET HAS BEEN SIGHTED OFF THE NORMANDY COAST! AND WE'VE BEEN PICKING UP STRANGE SIGNALS ON ALL THE ALLIED FREQUENCIES!
♪ HITLER! HAS ONLY GOT ONE BALL!

♪ THE OTHER! IS IN THE AL-BERT HALL!
♪ HIMMLER! HAS SOME-THING SIM'LAR!
♫ BUT POOR OLD GOEBBELS, HAS NO BALLS, AT ALL!
WH-WH-WHAT DOES IT MEAN, MEIN FUHRER?

IT MEANS MY GOOSE IS COOKED!

WHITE CLIFFS OF DOVER AHEAD, SIR!

BLOODY GOOD SHOW, DOUBTFUL...!

BLOODY GOOD SHOW.

OPERATION
BOLLOCK
AMMO

IN A TIME OF WAR...
IN A WORLD TORN APART BY THE UNSTOPPABLE MIGHT OF THE NAZI JUGGERNAUT...
ONE MADMAN, HIS LEFT TESTICLE MISSING SINCE BIRTH, HAS BROUGHT HUMANITY TO THE BRINK OF DESTRUCTION.
NOW, THAT TESTICLE, AND THE POWER WITHIN ITS HAIRY CIRCLE, WILL PUSH US ALL BEYOND THAT BRINK--AND ONLY A SMALL BAND OF WARRIORS WILL STAND BETWEEN FREEDOM AND A WORLD OF HELL.

BACK TO BLIGHTY

GERMAN-OCCUPIED GERMANY, SEPTEMBER 1944:
EY-OOP!
YER AHT OF ORDAH!
GAWD DAMMIT!
SETTLE DOWN, YOU MEN...

WELCOME BACK, CAPTAIN DARCY. AND YOU, LIEUTENANT MILK. WE'LL BE UNDER WAY IN JUST A MOMENT.
I SAY, LET'S NOT BEETLE OFF JUST YET, COMMANDER! STAY AND WATCH THE FIRE-WORKS, WHAT!

GAD, YES! ALWAYS A PLEASURE TO SEE A JOB WELL DONE!
MY CHAPS ARE THE BEST IN THE BUSINESS, DON'T Y'KNOW. NOTHING SARN'T CRUMB AND CORPORAL GEEZER LIKE MORE THAN BUMPING OFF A BRACE OR TWO OF JERRY GUARDS--NOTHING THE PIPER LIKES MORE THAN PIPING US ON OUR STEALTHY AND SECRETIVE WAY...

AND HANK THE YANK--ABSOLUTE GENIUS WITH EXPLOSIVES! WHY, WHO ELSE COULD SET THE CHARGES SO PRECISELY AS TO COMPLETELY OBLITERATE THAT GESTAPO HEADQUARTERS UP THERE WITHOUT EVEN SCRATCHING THE OLD PEOPLE'S RETIREMENT HOME NEXT DOOR...
WATCH THIS, COMMAND-ER--AND GET READY TO RAISE A ROUSING CHEER! A CHEER FOR THE--

RIFLE BRIGADE...

EY-OOP!
YER AHT OF ORDAH!
GAWD DAMMIT! GAWD DAMMIT! GAWD DAMMIT!

WE...
WE SEEM TO HAVE PUT UP RATHER A LARGE BLACK, SIR...
CHRIIIISST...!

LONDON:
CAPTAIN DARCY TO SEE COLONEL FRIGPIPE...

GOOD AFTERNOON, SIR.
WHAT-HO, HUGO! SPIFFING TO SEE YOU AGAIN!
THAT'LL BE ALL, CORPORAL...

SO, BLOTTED YOUR COPYBOOK, eh? SUITABLY PENITENT, I HOPE! SACKCLOTH AND ASHES AND ALL THAT SORT OF THING!
YES, WELL, IT WAS ALL REALLY RATHER A GHASTLY ACCIDENT, SIR. ABSOLUTELY FILTHY LUCK, I DON'T KNOW WHAT ELSE TO SAY...

WELL, NEVER MIND! HERE'S YOUR CHANCE TO REDEEM YOURSELF!
ANY IDEA WHAT THIS MIGHT BE...?

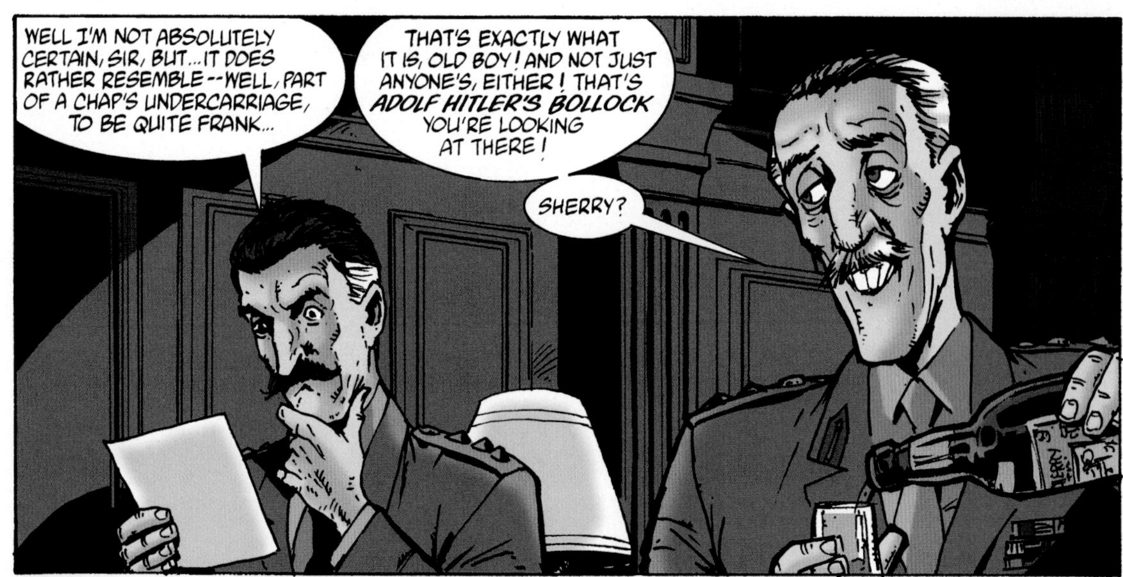
WELL I'M NOT ABSOLUTELY CERTAIN, SIR, BUT...IT DOES RATHER RESEMBLE--WELL, PART OF A CHAP'S UNDERCARRIAGE, TO BE QUITE FRANK...
THAT'S EXACTLY WHAT IT IS, OLD BOY! AND NOT JUST ANYONE'S, EITHER! THAT'S ADOLF HITLER'S BOLLOCK YOU'RE LOOKING AT THERE!
SHERRY?

OH, RATHER. SO THIS REALLY IS THE BLIGHTER'S BALL, THEN?
THE HEAD NAZI'S KNACKER! YOUR ACTUAL TEUTONIC TESTICLE!

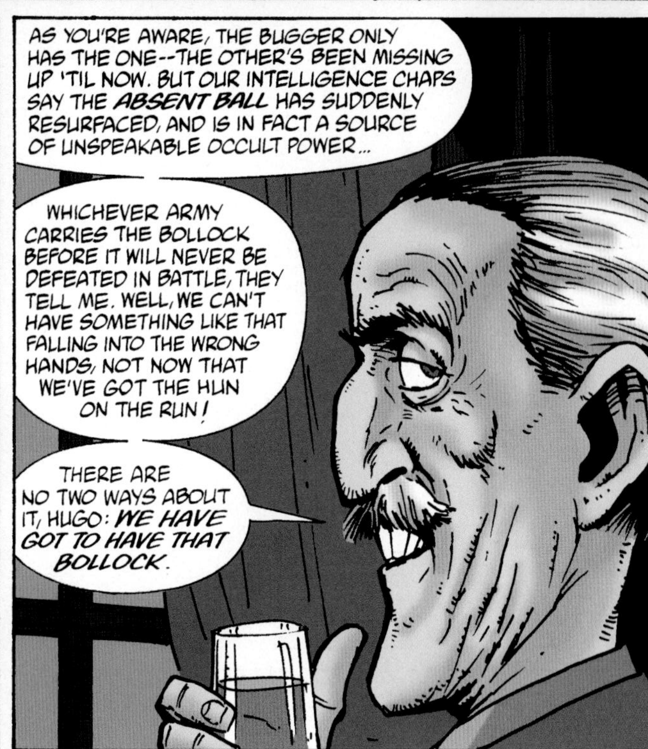
AS YOU'RE AWARE, THE BUGGER ONLY HAS THE ONE--THE OTHER'S BEEN MISSING UP 'TIL NOW. BUT OUR INTELLIGENCE CHAPS SAY THE ABSENT BALL HAS SUDDENLY RESURFACED, AND IS IN FACT A SOURCE OF UNSPEAKABLE OCCULT POWER...
WHICHEVER ARMY CARRIES THE BOLLOCK BEFORE IT WILL NEVER BE DEFEATED IN BATTLE, THEY TELL ME. WELL, WE CAN'T HAVE SOMETHING LIKE THAT FALLING INTO THE WRONG HANDS, NOT NOW THAT WE'VE GOT THE HUN ON THE RUN!
THERE ARE NO TWO WAYS ABOUT IT, HUGO: WE HAVE GOT TO HAVE THAT BOLLOCK.

HAVE YOU TRIED THE ALBERT HALL, SIR?
FIRST PLACE WE LOOKED, OLD MAN.

NO, THE DASHED THING'S BEEN TRACKED TO SEMMEN, A LITTLE COUNTRY OVER IN JOHNNY ARAB'S NECK OF THE WOODS. WE HAVEN'T BEEN ABLE TO CONFIRM THIS, BUT IT MAY IN FACT BE IN THE POSSESSION OF THE LOCAL SULTAN...
MARVELOUS PLACE, SEMMEN. USED TO HUNT THERE BEFORE THE WAR. GOT ATTACKED BY A LION AT ONE POINT.

A LION, SIR?
CAME AS RATHER A SHOCK, ACTUALLY... I WAS MAKING MY WAY ALONG A WADI, IN SEARCH OF ONE OF THE LOCAL GOATS FOR A SPOT OF THE OLD YOU-KNOW-WHAT, WHEN THE BLASTED ANIMAL LEAPT OUT AT ME AND WENT--

RRRAAAAARRR!!

FOULED MY BRITCHES, I'M SORRY TO SAY.
OH, I--I SAY, SIR... WHAT FRIGHTFULLY BAD LUCK...
AND THE LION?

WELL OBVIOUSLY I SHOT IT... NO, NO, IT WAS ONLY JUST NOW GOING RRAAARR THAT I FOULED MY BREECHES...
ANYWAY, I WANT THE RIFLE BRIGADE ON THE VERY NEXT FLIGHT TO SEMMEN. HAVE A WORD WITH OUR CHAP AT THE EMBASSY, FIND OUT THE LIE OF THE LAND--
AND GET THAT BOLLOCK, HUGO.

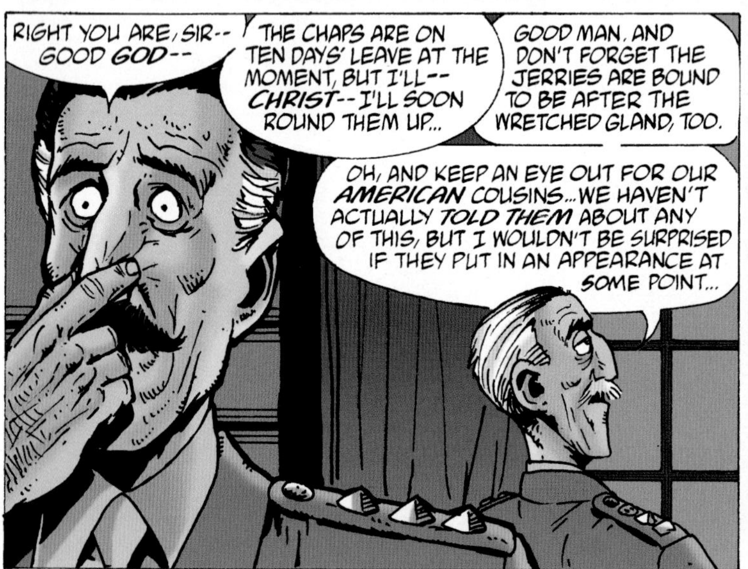
RIGHT YOU ARE, SIR-- GOOD GOD--
THE CHAPS ARE ON TEN DAYS' LEAVE AT THE MOMENT, BUT I'LL-- CHRIST-- I'LL SOON ROUND THEM UP...
GOOD MAN. AND DON'T FORGET THE JERRIES ARE BOUND TO BE AFTER THE WRETCHED GLAND, TOO.
OH, AND KEEP AN EYE OUT FOR OUR AMERICAN COUSINS... WE HAVEN'T ACTUALLY TOLD THEM ABOUT ANY OF THIS, BUT I WOULDN'T BE SURPRISED IF THEY PUT IN AN APPEARANCE AT SOME POINT...

NOW: YOU HAVE YOUR ORDERS, CAPTAIN.
OPERATION BOLLOCK IS ON.

GOLGOTHA HOUSE, ESSEX:
GOOD TO SEE YOU AGAIN, MASTER HUGO. STAYING LONG?
JUST A FLYING VISIT, CLITTERS. HERE TO COLLECT THE PIPER.
F O DT

I SAY, THAT'S NEW...
MASTER ROBERT IS ALSO WITH US AT PRESENT, SIR.

BROTHER BOBBY.
OH, **SUPER**.
HUGO, YOU OLD SHIRT-LIFTER!

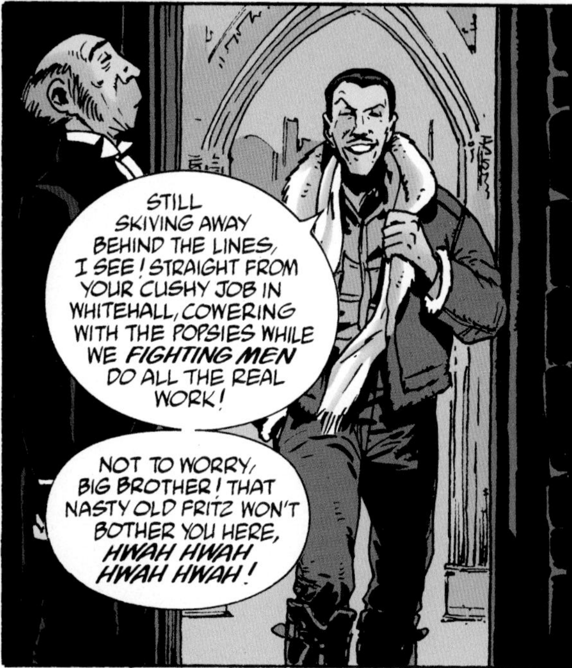

STILL SKIVING AWAY BEHIND THE LINES, I SEE! STRAIGHT FROM YOUR CUSHY JOB IN WHITEHALL, COWERING WITH THE POPSIES WHILE WE **FIGHTING MEN** DO ALL THE REAL WORK!
NOT TO WORRY, BIG BROTHER! THAT NASTY OLD FRITZ WON'T BOTHER YOU HERE, **HWAH HWAH HWAH HWAH!**

WHAT A PLEASANT SURPRISE TO FIND YOU HERE, BOBBY. AN ABSOLUTE TREAT.
GOT A HEINKEL LAST NIGHT--PERFECT FLAMER, NOT THAT FAR FROM HERE! THOUGHT I'D DROP IN ON THE OLD MATER AND PATER, WHAT?
ONE SNAG, THOUGH--HAD RATHER A LOT TO DRINK AT DINNER, STILL UTTERLY SOZZLED WHEN I GOT THE JERRY, FORGOT ALL ABOUT THE UNDERCART LEVER AND PRANGED THE OLD SPIT ON THE LAWN!

AND SPEAKING OF THAT SORT OF THING--
OH GOD, HOW DREARY.
MUMMY'S *PISSED* AGAIN.

IS IT THE *GERMANS*, BOBBY?
IT'S ONLY HUGO, MUMMY.

LET THEM INVADE! THEY CAN RAVISH ME! *RAVISH ME!* BY GOD, WE'LL SEE WHO BREAKS FIRST!
I SHALL OFFER MYSELF, *SACRIFICE MYSELF* IN GALLANT DEFENSE OF MY COUNTRY! WHOLE *PANZER DIVISIONS* WILL DISAPPEAR IN THE STYGIAN DEPTHS OF MY ORIFICES!
YES, THAT'S LOVELY, MUMMY...
I'LL LEAVE YOU TO IT, OLD CHAP! SURELY EVEN A DESKBOUND NANCY BOY LIKE YOU CAN HANDLE THIS ONE, *HWAH HWAH HWAH HWAH*!

DASH IT ALL! IF MY WORK WITH THE RIFLE BRIGADE WASN'T CLASSIFIED **TOP SECRET** I'D SOON SHOW BOBBY A THING OR TWO--INSTEAD I'M FORCED TO ENDURE HIS ENDLESS BARBS AND INSULTS!

OF COURSE, I CAN TELL YOU, MUMMY, BECAUSE YOU'RE SUCH AN AWFUL OLD GIN-SOAKED LUSH YOU WON'T REMEMBER ANYWAY...
RAVISH ME, I TELL YOU! I SHALL ADD THEIR NAMES TO MY **ENORMOUS CATALOGUE** OF LOVERS!

HHHHH.
I'LL JUST LOOK IN ON DADDY.

OVER THE TOP! **OVER THE TOP!**
HAND GRENADES, THEY SAID! **ARTILLERY,** THEY SAID! **MACHINE-GUNS AND BARBED WIRE,** THEY SAID!
STUFF AND NONSENSE! **POPPY-COCK,** I TOLD THEM! THE HUN WON'T LOOK SO CLEVER WHEN WE GO IN WITH THE COLD STEEL...

WELL THANK GOD **SOMEBODY'S** NORMAL.

THIS JERRY BOMBER THAT BOBBY CLAIMS TO HAVE DESTROYED, CLITTERS--ANY IDEA WHAT HAPPENED TO THE CREW?
MASTER ROBERT SAID THEY TOOK TO THEIR PARACHUTES, SIR. HE BELIEVES THEY CAME DOWN SOMEWHERE IN THE GROUNDS OF THE ESTATE.

WHICH MEANS THE PIPER HAS THEM.
IN THE *MIDDEN*.
I'LL NEVER TEMPT HIM OUT NOW, UNLESS ...COOKY?

YESH, YOUNG MASHTER?
FETCH ME A HAGGIS.
YESH, YOUNG MASHTER.

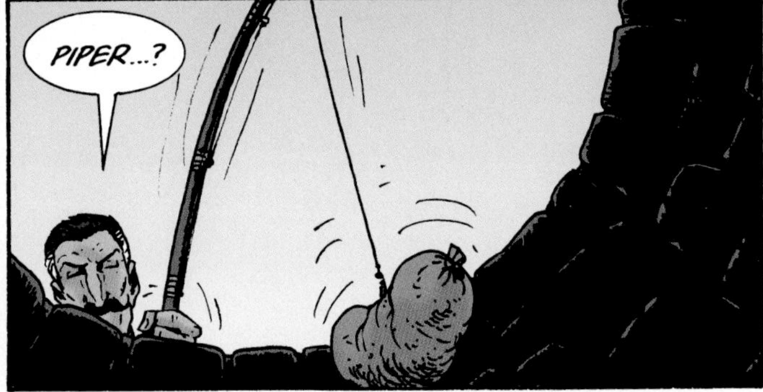
PIPER...?

PIPER...!

NFF NFF

NFF NFF

GAH--!
UP YOU COME--THAT'S THE WAY--

GOOD MAN, PIPER! READY FOR THE OFF, I HOPE!

THRAIP, EAST YORKSHIRE:
ROLL OOP! ROLL OOP FOR BATTLE O' FOOKIN' TITANS!
The Brick Shithouse

BY 'ECK, GET ON WI' IT, LAD!
SETTLE DOWN, LADS! PLACE YER BETS!
GODDAMN LIMEYS!
EXCUSE ME, BUT WHAT'S THAT STAR ON THE WALL FOR?
THAT'S ENOOF! THAT'S ENOOF!
FRIENDLY INVASION MY FOOKIN' ARSE!

IN'T BLOO CORNER--SOME FOOKIN' YANK PUFF FROM ARMY BASE OVER 'ILL!
WUURRRGGHH! WUUNNNGHH!

IN'T RED CORNER--
EY-OOP!

SECONDS AWAY--
ROUND FOOKIN'
ONE!
WUUNNGGHH!
UH UVUH TUGUH!
UH UVUH
TUGUH!

EY-
OOP!
WHAM

EY-OOP!
SORRY
TO INTERRUPT,
SARN'T CRUMB--

BUT THE
RIFLE BRIGADE
WANTS YOU.
ADRIENNnnne...

DAHN THE EAST END:
SPECIAL OPERATIONS OR NOT, CAPTAIN DARCY, EXPOSING ONE'S BUTTOCKS TO A MEMBER OF THE ROYAL FAMILY IS A VERY SERIOUS MATTER!
POLICE

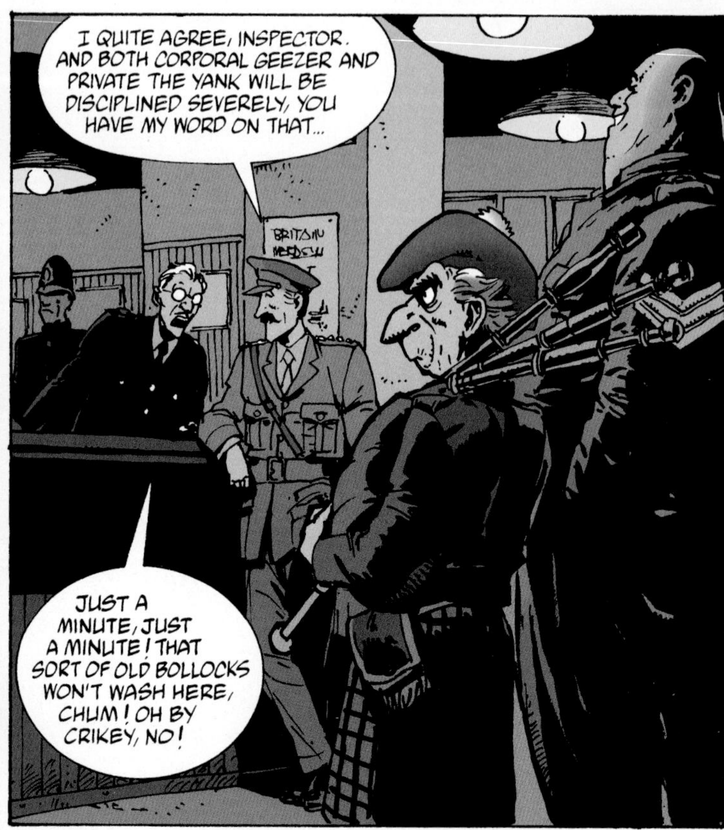
I QUITE AGREE, INSPECTOR. AND BOTH CORPORAL GEEZER AND PRIVATE THE YANK WILL BE DISCIPLINED SEVERELY, YOU HAVE MY WORD ON THAT...
JUST A MINUTE, JUST A MINUTE! THAT SORT OF OLD BOLLOCKS WON'T WASH HERE, CHUM! OH BY CRIKEY, NO!

I WAS IN HONG KONG BEFORE THE WAR, MATEY! SHANGHAI! SINGAPORE! I KNOW YOU ARMY WALLAHS OF OLD!
YOU COME WALTZING IN HERE, SHOUTING ABOUT OPERATIONAL NECESSITY AND PERSONNEL VITAL TO THE SUCCESS OF THIS, THAT, AND THE OTHER, DEMANDING THE RELEASE OF YOUR HOOLIGANS FROM MY CELLS? OH BY CRIKEY NO, SUNSHINE!
THE CHINESE HAVE AN OLD SAYING: "BEWARE THE CHERRY BLOSSOM HELD IN THE CLAWS OF THE TIGER!" SO PUT THAT IN YOUR PIPE AND SMOKE IT!

QUITE.
I'M NOT DEMANDING ANYONE'S RELEASE, INSPECTOR. I'M SIMPLY HERE TO PICK UP MY CHAPS WHEN THEY ARRANGE THEIR OWN.

FOOOOM
LUMME!
BLIMEY!

YER AHT OF ORDAH!
GAWD DAMMIT!
BLOODY GOOD SHOW, CHAPS!

YOU WON'T BE NEEDING THE HOSTAGE, CORPORAL...
YOU BLITHERING INCOMPETENT! HOW THE HELL DID THEY GET KNIVES AND EXPLOSIVES INTO THEIR CELL?
THEY MUST'VE SMUGGLED 'EM IN, SAH! CONCEALED 'EM UP THE OL' BACK PASSAGE!

YOU HAVEN'T HEARD THE LAST OF THIS, DARCY! THOSE TWO SAVAGES OF YOURS GAVE HIS MAJESTY A FACE-FUL OF BROWNEYE!
I'LL NICK THE BLOODY PAIR OF THEM, OH BY CRIKEY I WILL!
THE CHINESE HAVE ANOTHER OLD SAYING, INSPECTOR:

"DREAM ON, YOU FOUR-EYED CUNT."

BUNNYDOWN WATERS, SHROPSHIRE:
HELLO, UNCLE JIMMY!
MORNING, CECIL.
I'M GLAD I RAN INTO YOU, OLD CHAP. I WAS HOPING WE COULD HAVE A BIT OF A *CHAT*...

LOVELY DAY, *eh?* ABSOLUTELY FIRST CLASS.
SORT OF DAY A FELLOW MIGHT WANT TO SPEND WITH, WELL, I DON'T KNOW, A LOVELY YOUNG LADY, PERHAPS...
WHY WOULD THAT BE, UNCLE JIMMY?

WELL THAT'S...SORT OF WHAT I WANTED TO TALK TO YOU ABOUT, OLD MAN...

AS YOU KNOW, ON THE NIGHT BEFORE THEY HANGED THEMSELVES, YOUR MOTHER AND FATHER MADE YOUR AUNT FRAGRANCE AND ME PROMISE WE'D LOOK AFTER YOU. AND, WELL, ONCE WE'RE GONE YOU'LL BE THE LAST OF THE MILKS, OLD CHAP, THE LINE REALLY DOES END WITH YOU, AND WE WERE WONDERING ABOUT, WELL, THE NEXT GENERATION, AS IT WERE, AND WITH YOU NOT REALLY...*EVER*...HAVING BROUGHT A YOUNG LADY HOME FOR TEA, WE WERE...WE...
LOOK, YOU DON'T...OH GOD, YOU DON'T PREFER *CHAPS* OR...OR...
OR ANY-THING...LIKE *THAT*, DO YOU...?

PREFER CHAPS FOR WHAT, UNCLE JIMMY?

OH CHRIST.
IT'S...IT'S A QUESTION OF...YOU KNOW, OF SNAILS OR OYSTERS, AH, I DON'T KNOW IF I CAN PUT IT MUCH CLEARER THAN THAT--
CAN YOU HEAR SOME-THING, UNCLE JIMMY?

YER AHT OF ORDAH!
EY-OOP!
GAWD DAMMIT!
WHAT-HO, DOUBTFUL! READY FOR SOME RED-HOT ACTION WITH MYSELF AND THE CHAPS?

WHAT?
OH, TOP HOLE!
I'M READY! TAKE ME, MY CAPTAIN, MY CAPTAIN!

BACK ON OPS AT LAST, SIR?
TRIFLE TOO HUSH-HUSH TO DISCUSS IN FRONT OF CIVILIANS, DOUBTFUL --BUT I CAN DEFINITELY PROMISE YOU SOME ROUGH STUFF!
WHAT?

LET'S GO AND GIVE IT TO 'EM, THEN!
PIPER-- COCK O' THE GLENS!

NO-NEE-NI-NO-NEE-NO-NAR
WHAT?

ENTERING SEMMENI AIRSPACE NOW, CAPTAIN DARCY. SHOULD REACH SIDI BOOMBOOM AIRPORT BY OH-NINE-HUNDRED.

GOOD SHOW, PILOT!
ONCE THERE WE'LL MAKE OUR WAY TO THE EMBASSY. SHOULD ALL BE PLAIN SAILING UP 'TIL THEN, AT LEAST.
I'M EVER SO GLAD TO HEAR THAT, SIR...

SO, OUR INTELLIGENCE WAS CORRECT--THE RIFLE BRIGADE ARE RIGHT ON TIME! LITTLE DO THEY SUSPECT THE *DOOM* THAT AWAITS THEM IN THE DESERT SKIES!
AT LAST I SHALL ELIMINATE THE SCHWEINE WHO COMMITTED THAT *FOUL CRIME* AGAINST MY FAMILY--

AT LAST I SHALL HAVE MY *REVENGE!*
BLOODY HELL! *FOCKE WULF AT TWO O'CLOCK!*

I SAY! FEELS LIKE A SPOT OF TURBULENCE, WHAT!

PILOT! HOLD HER *STEADY*, BLAST YOU!
THAT ISN'T TURBULENCE! *THE STARBOARD ENGINE'S ON FIRE!*

AUF WIEDERSEHEN, ENGLANDER RABBLE! THE BETTER MAN WON, HEIN?
GRAB THE CONTROLS, DOUBTFUL! YOU'RE GOING TO HAVE TO LAND THE BRUTE!

OH, THIS IS *UTTERLY BEASTLY*--!
IT'S ALL UP TO YOU NOW, LIEUTENANT! THE REST OF US ARE COUNTING ON YOU!

TELL THE CHAPS TO BRACE THEMSELVES, SIR!
I'M GOING TO DO--THE BEST--I CAN--

BLOODY GOOD EFFORT, DOUBTFUL!

DOUBTFUL?
DOUBTFUL, OLD BOY! SPEAK UP!
O...OVER HERE...

DOUBTFUL--!
LOOKS LIKE I'VE... BOUGHT IT, SIR...

DON'T TRY AND MOVE, OLD CHAP!
WOULDN'T... WOULDN'T MAKE MUCH DIFFERENCE NOW, CAPTAIN...
CHRIST, THE HORROR! THERE MUST BE SOME WAY TO-- TO EASE THE PAIN!

WELL...NOW YOU COME TO MENTION IT...

ANYTHING, DOUBTFUL!
R...REALLY...?
ABSOLUTELY ANYTHING! IN HEAVEN'S NAME, JUST TELL ME WHAT TO DO!

THEN GIVE MY OLD CHAP A BIT OF A SUCK, SIR...
WHAT?!
LIKE... LIKE NANNY USED TO DO...

HAVE YOU TAKEN LEAVE OF YOUR SENSES, MAN? I'M NOT BALLY WELL DOING THAT!
ANYTHING, YOU SAID...
I HEAR WINGS...GREAT WINGS, BEATING SO SLOWLY...
CAN IT BE... THE ANGEL OF DEATH...?

OH MY GOD.
IT NEEDN'T BE SO BAD, SIR... PROBABLY JUST LIKE A SAUSAGE...

EY-OOP!
PERHAPS A BANANA--
WHAT THE BLAZES--?

THERE ISN'T EVEN A MARK ON YOU! THAT ISN'T YOUR ARM, IT MUST BE ONE OF THE PILOT'S!
GOOD LORD, SO IT MUST! ISN'T IT FUNNY THE TRICKS YOUR MIND CAN PLAY ON YOU!

BUT...IF...
HMMM.

ALL RIGHT, CHAPS; SIDIBOOMBOOM'S TEN MILES IN THAT DIRECTION. A BRISK STROLL SHOULD SEE US THERE BY NOON.

AND--
GAWD DAMMIT!
EY-OOP!
YER AHT OF ORDAH!
SO, OUR LUFTWAFFE HERO HAS FAILED IN HIS TASK...

THE ENGLANDER OAFS STILL LIVE!
BUT NOT FOR LONG! NOW THEY ENTER THE WEB OF DANGER AND DECEIT THAT I HAVE SPUN HERE IN SIDIBOOMBOOM--AND SOON THEY WILL DISCOVER THAT THE SEARCH FOR THE FUHRER'S GONAD BRINGS ONLY DEATH!

SOON MY VENGEANCE ON THE RIFLE BRIGADE WILL BE COMPLETE!
Next:
Raiders of the Lost Ball

GLENN
FABRY
APRIL 01

CAPTAIN DARCY AND THE RIFLE BRIGADE, I PRESUME. CARRINGTON-SHYTE OF THE F.O.
I WAS EXPECTING YOU A TRIFLE EARLIER...

YES, WELL WE RAN INTO A SPOT OF BOTHER ON THE FLIGHT IN. YOUR OFFICE AT THE EMBASSY SAID WE COULD FIND YOU HERE.
DID THEY? HOW HELPFUL OF THEM. NO DOUBT THEY CAN ALSO SUPPLY YOU WITH TRANSPORT, AND ANYTHING ELSE YOU NEED DURING YOUR TIME IN SIDI BOOMBOOM.
WHY DON'T YOU RUN ALONG NOW AND HAVE THEM KIT YOU OUT, MM?

LOOK HERE, YOU'RE SUPPOSED TO BE OUR LIAISON OFFICER! WE'RE HERE ON A TOP SECRET MISSION TO RECOVER HITLER'S TESTICLE FROM THE LOCAL SULTAN, AND YOU'RE SITTING HERE SMOKING JUJU WEED!
IN HEAVEN'S NAME, MAN, DON'T YOU KNOW THERE'S A WAR ON?
I'D HEARD A RUMOR TO THAT EFFECT. SADLY, MY FLAT FEET AND PERFORATED EAR-DRUM HAVE KEPT ME OUT OF THE ACTION.
AND IF YOU'RE LOOK-ING FOR THE SULTAN--

HE'S BEHIND YOU.
EY-OOP!
GAWD DAMMIT!
YER AHT OF ORDAH!

I AM ALI BEN RAJAPOOR RASHID O'KHAN, SULTAN OF SIDI BOOMBOOM AND THE LAND BEYOND ITS WALLS.
IN THE NAME OF ALLAH, I BID YOU WELCOME, MY ENGLISH FRIENDS--
WELCOME TO SEMMEN.
THE PEARLS OF ARABIA

CAPTAIN DARCY AND SECOND-LIEUTENANT MILK, COMMANDING THE RIFLE BRIGADE. SPLENDID *BEAST,* YOUR EXCELLENCY...
AH, MY BULL ELEPHANT, *M'BUBBA!* BROUGHT HERE AS A CALF FROM THE DISTANT JUNGLES OF AFRICA!

FOR FIVE SCORE YEARS AND TEN HAS M'BUBBA SERVED MY FAMILY! HE IS MY GREATEST AND MOST PRIZED POSSESSION, MORE PRECIOUS EVEN THAN MY WIVES AND CHILDREN!
LOUD INDEED ARE HIS WARLIKE BELLOWS, AS HE LEADS MY ARMIES INTO BATTLE! LONG AND LOW ARE THE MOANS OF THE COWS OF HIS HERD, AS HE UNLEASHES HIS ALMIGHTY SHLONG!
EY-OOP!

AH...YES, THAT'S VERY... AH...
A WORD TO THE WISE, DARCY EFFENDI! ANY MAN WHO SEEKS THE GOOLIE OF THE GREAT DICTATOR WOULD DO WELL TO ATTEND THE BANQUET I AM THROWING AT MY GRAND PALACE THIS VERY EVE!

THERE WE WILL DISCUSS BOLLOCKS...
AMONG OTHER THINGS.

RATHER AN ODD CHAP, THIS SULTAN, SIR...
MORE THAN ODD, DOUBTFUL--RUM! DOWNRIGHT RUM! AND HE'S NOT THE ONLY RUM THING AROUND HERE!

HOW DID FRITZ KNOW WE WERE COMING? THE LUFT-WAFFE WERE KICKED OUT OF THE MIDDLE EAST TWO YEARS AGO, BUT THAT JERRY FIGHTER KNEW EXACTLY WHERE TO INTERCEPT US!
HAVE SAR'NT CRUMB BRING UP THE VEHICLE THE EMBASSY WALLAHS GAVE US. TIME WE HAD A BIT OF A SHUFTI ROUND SIDI BOOMBOOM...

BACK IN A TRICE, SIR.
WHERE'S THAT CARRINGTON-SHYTE FELLOW WANDERED OFF TO? I WANTED A WORD WITH--

GOOD GOD--!
DEATH TO THE INFIDEL!

HOW DARE YOU, SIR!
AAAAH! SCHWEINER ENGLANDER!

I MEAN-- INFIDEL DOG! SON OF A SCORPION!
INFIDEL NOTHING! YOU'RE A KRAUT!

VERDAMMT, VERDAMMT! I'M OFF!
STOP HIM! STOP THAT MAN!

SCHIESSE!
YER AHT OF ORDAH!
GAWD DAMMIT!
NOW...I'M AFRAID WE'RE GOING TO HAVE TO HAVE A LITTLE CHAT...

AAAAIIIEEEE!!

GET IN HERE, YOU FOOL! SCHNELL!
THEY'RE GETTING AWAY, SIR!
DAMN AND BLAST IT! I WANTED THAT JERRY FOR INTERROGATION!

EY-OOP!
IT'S SAR'NT CRUMB WITH THE TRANSPORT!
ABSOLUTELY SPIFFING! GAD, WE'LL SOON RUN THE BLIGHTER TO EARTH!
BY THE CHOCOLATE STARFISH OF ALLAH--!
YOU HAD NO ORDERS TO ATTACK THE ENGLANDER, DAMN YOU! YOU COULD HAVE GIVEN AWAY OUR ENTIRE OPERATION!
I HAD NO CHOICE, HERR LEUTNANT! HE ALMOST BLUNDERED INTO OUR NUMBER ONE AGENT!
FULL SPEED AHEAD, SAR'NT!
READY THE GUNS! STAND BY TO ENGAGE THE ENEMY!
PIPER-- JOCK THE ARAB!

NEE-NAR-NI-NO-NO-NAR-NEE

BRITISH ENGINEERING--FINEST IN THE WORLD! THE HUN WON'T STAND A CHANCE!

OPEN FIRE, CORPORAL! AIM FOR THE TIRES, THAT OUGHT TO CRAMP HIS STYLE!

GAWD DAMMIT!
YER AHT OF ORDAH!
WHAT THE BLAZES WAS *THAT?*

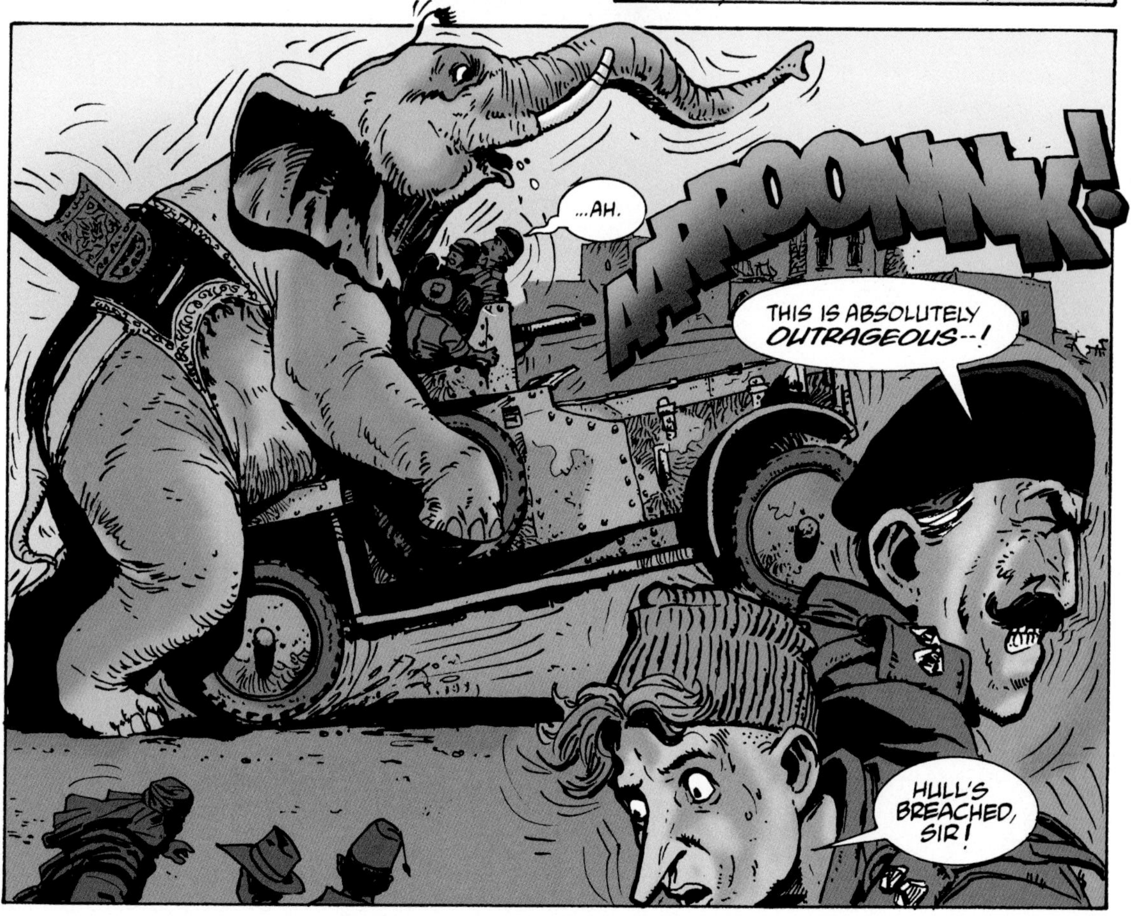

...AH.
AARROONNNK!
THIS IS ABSOLUTELY *OUTRAGEOUS*--!
HULL'S BREACHED, SIR!

YER AHT OF ORDAH!
I--I REALLY DON'T CARE FOR THIS--!
STEADY, LIEUTENANT! THE LOCALS ARE WATCHING!
EY-OOP!
GAWD DAMMIT!

BE BRITISH! REMEMBER THE STIFF UPPER LIP!
AROONK!

ARONK! ARONK! ARONK!
SHOULDN'T BE LONG NOW, CHAPS! PREPARE TO RECOMMENCE PURSUIT!

AARONNK!
ENGINE'S FLOODED, SIR!
OH, CONFOUND THE LUCK!

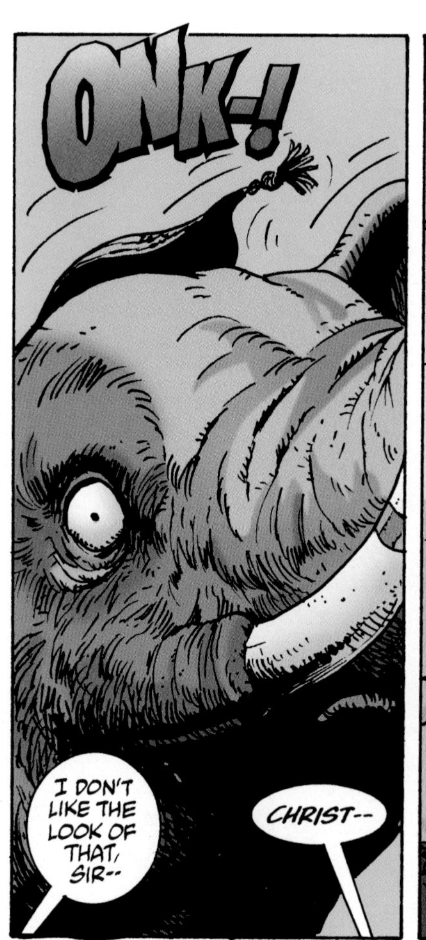
ONK-!
I DON'T LIKE THE LOOK OF THAT, SIR--
CHRIST--

BAIL OUT, YOU CHAPS!
KRUNCH!

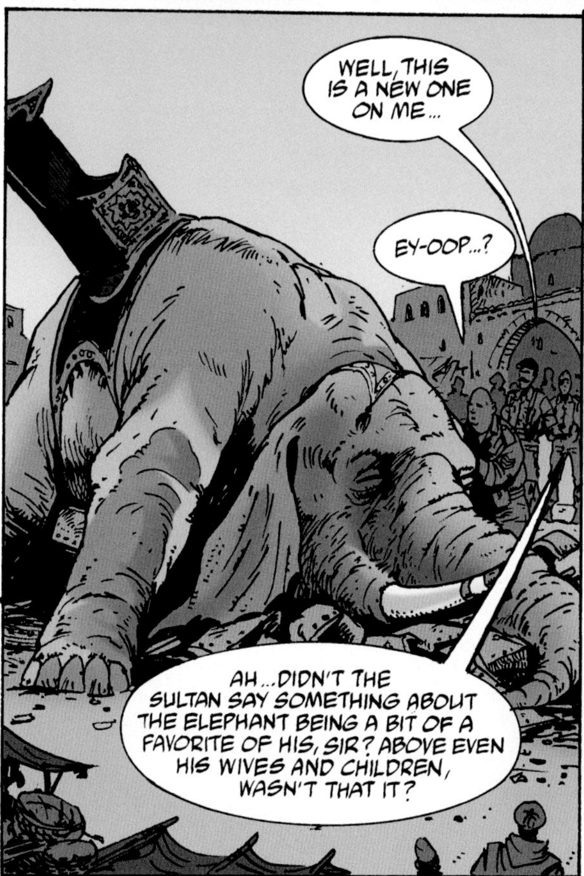
WELL, THIS IS A NEW ONE ON ME...
EY-OOP...?
AH...DIDN'T THE SULTAN SAY SOMETHING ABOUT THE ELEPHANT BEING A BIT OF A FAVORITE OF HIS, SIR? ABOVE EVEN HIS WIVES AND CHILDREN, WASN'T THAT IT?

GOOD POINT, DOUBTFUL. MIGHTN'T BE A BAD IDEA TO MAKE OURSELVES SCARCE.
AIRCRAFT IN THE SUN, SIR!

PROBABLY A SPIT FROM OUR AIRFIELD AT MERSA BEDARDI. THIS IS HARDLY THE TIME FOR PLANE-SPOTTING, DOUBTFUL...
THAT'S NO SPITFIRE--
IT'S A FOCKE WULF ONE-NINETY AAAAHH!!
DEATH TO THE RIFLE BRIGADE!
IT'S THE SOD THAT SHOT US DOWN THE LAST TIME!
TAKE COVER!!
SO, THE SCHWEINEHUNDEN SURVIVED MY LAST ATTACK! THIS TIME I SHALL MAKE SURE OF THEM!
THIS TIME--MY VENGEANCE SHALL BE COMPLETE!

DONNER UND BLITZEN!
PISS-POOR EFFORT, FRITZ! NO COCONUT FOR YOU!

NEXT TIME, ENGLANDERS! NEXT TIME!
TREAT THE SWINE WITH THE CONTEMPT THEY DESERVE, THAT'S WHAT I SAY... EVERYONE ALL RIGHT?

EVERYONE... BUT ME, SIR...
DOUBTFUL--!

COPPED A PACKET... RIGHT IN THE BREAD BASKET...
NO!
SO STRANGE... I ALWAYS EXPECTED TO DIE... IN ENGLAND...

NOT LIKE THIS, DOUBTFUL! NOT THIS GHASTLY, LINGERING AGONY!
DEAR GOD IN HEAVEN, THERE MUST BE SOME-THING I CAN DO!

WELL...
YES?
YOU COULD...
YES?
TELL ME, DOUBTFUL! ANYTHING YOU WANT, A DYING MAN'S LAST WISH!

THEN GIVE ME A GOOD HARD ROGERING, SIR...
LIKE NANNY USED TO DO...

YOU'VE ABSOLUTELY GOT TO BE JOKING--
IS THAT... YOU, GOD...?

OH NO.
SHOW ME THE LOVE OF TIGERS, SIR...

FIFTY JILDAR!
Eh?
FIFTY JILDAR FOR TOMATO!

YOU MUST PAY FOR TOMATO! FIFTY JILDAR!
BUT YOU SAID YOU'D BEEN SHOT IN THE STOMACH! LIEUTENANT MILK, WHAT THE HELL IS GOING ON HERE?

OH DEAR, SILLY OLD ME! WHAT AN IDIOT I AM!
I MUST HAVE STUMBLED AGAINST THIS FELLOW'S STALL AND CRUSHED THE TOMATO WHEN THE JERRY FIGHTER ATTACKED US! OH WELL, THE EYE SEES WHAT IT EXPECTS TO SEE, I SUPPOSE!
BUT--
BUT--!

HMMMM.

VERY WELL, AH...THIS BUNFIGHT THE SULTAN'S THROWING WOULD SEEM TO BE OUR BEST BET FOR FINDING THE BOLLOCK. BACK TO THE EMBASSY TO CHANGE, THEN ON TO THE GRAND PALACE...
YES, ENGLANDERS...!

ON TO THE PALACE-- AND INTO MY TRAP!
THE HOUR OF MY REVENGE DRAWS EVER CLOSER!

SO, A BUNCH OF GODDAMN LIMEYS, HUH?

YOU BOYS CAME FOR AY-DOLF'S BALL, YOU MAY AS WELL QUIT AN' GO HOME! UNCLE SAM'S TOP MAN IS ON THE CASE!
MARYLAND SMITH IS THE NAME-- ADVENTURE, INTRIGUE AN' CHASIN' TAIL IS THE GAME!
I THINK THAT'S THREE GAMES...

GOOD POINT, DOUBTFUL. ARE THE GAMES, NOT IS THE GAME...
DON'T GET GRAMMATICAL WITH ME, TEA-SIPPER!

I SAY, MARY, CALM DOWN--
AND DON'T FUCKING CALL ME MARY!

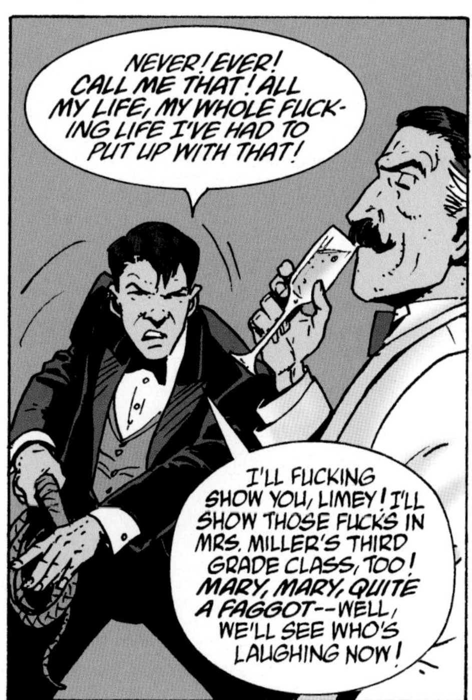
NEVER! EVER! CALL ME THAT! ALL MY LIFE, MY WHOLE FUCKING LIFE I'VE HAD TO PUT UP WITH THAT!
I'LL FUCKING SHOW YOU, LIMEY! I'LL SHOW THOSE FUCKS IN MRS. MILLER'S THIRD GRADE CLASS, TOO! MARY, MARY, QUITE A FAGGOT--WELL, WE'LL SEE WHO'S LAUGHING NOW!

KE-RAKK
EEEIGGHH!!

JESUS! FUCK! FUCK! JESUS!
DINNER IS SERVED, LADIES AND GENTLEMEN!
A WORD IN YOUR EAR, CARRINGTON-SHYTE...

WHAT'S AN AMERICAN DOING LOOKING FOR THE BOLLOCK? BRITAIN'S SUPPORTED SEMMEN FOR CENTURIES, THEY'RE ONLY SUPPOSED TO HAVE TOLD US--HOW THE BLAZES DID WASHINGTON FIND OUT?
NO ONE IS MORE SHOCKED THAN I, CAPTAIN. SECURITY ON YOUR OPERATION'S BEEN ABSOLUTELY TIP-TOP, I SAW TO IT PERSONALLY.
HOW OUR GALLANT ALLIES GOT WIND OF THE GONAD I REALLY CAN'T IMAGINE...

GALLANT ALLIES MY ASS! THE ARMY THAT CARRIES THE TESTICLE CAN NEVER BE DEFEATED--WELL THAT AIN'T GONNA BE THOSE FUCKERS, I'M GONNA MAKE GODDAMN SURE OF IT!
THE BALL BELONGS TO UNCLE SAM!

GREETINGS, MY FRIENDS! ALI BEN RAJAPOOR RASHID O'KHAN BIDS YOU WELCOME TO HIS TABLE!

AS SOME OF YOU ALREADY KNOW, TONIGHT'S CELEBRATION IS TOUCHED BY DEEPEST SORROW. MY GREAT BULL ELEPHANT, M'BUBBA, WAS FOUND DEAD THIS VERY DAY IN THE MARKET QUARTER.
IF ANY WERE RESPONSIBLE FOR THIS TERRIBLE THING, THEY HAVE YET TO REVEAL THEMSELVES...

BUT, AS A MARK OF RESPECT FOR THIS MOST NOBLE CREATURE, I HAVE ORDAINED THAT WE SHALL DINE ON HIS FLESH THIS VERY NIGHT!
MAY HIS BOUNDLESS STRENGTH SUSTAIN US! MAY HIS MEMORY LIVE FOREVER IN OUR HEARTS!
ROAST JUMBO, EH? I'LL TRY ANYTHING ONCE!
SO LONG AS HE STOPS WITTERING ON, SIR! I'M ABSOLUTELY STARVING!

TO OUR ENGLISH GUESTS, OF COURSE--
WE OFFER ONLY THE TASTIEST PORTION.

AH...WOULD THIS BE M'BUBBA'S TRUNK, YOUR EXCELLENCY?

NO, CAPTAIN.
NOT HIS TRUNK.

YOU REALLY MUST EAT IT, OLD CHAP. FRIGHTFUL BREACH OF ETIQUETTE IF YOU DON'T.
BON APPETIT...

AND...
NOT BAD, ACTUALLY. SORT OF GAMEY, YOU MIGHT SAY...
I WOULD NOT WISH TO INTERRUPT YOUR ENJOYMENT OF THE FOOD, MY FRIENDS--

BUT YOU MIGHT LIKE TO FEAST YOUR EYES ON THIS.
THE BOLLOCK!

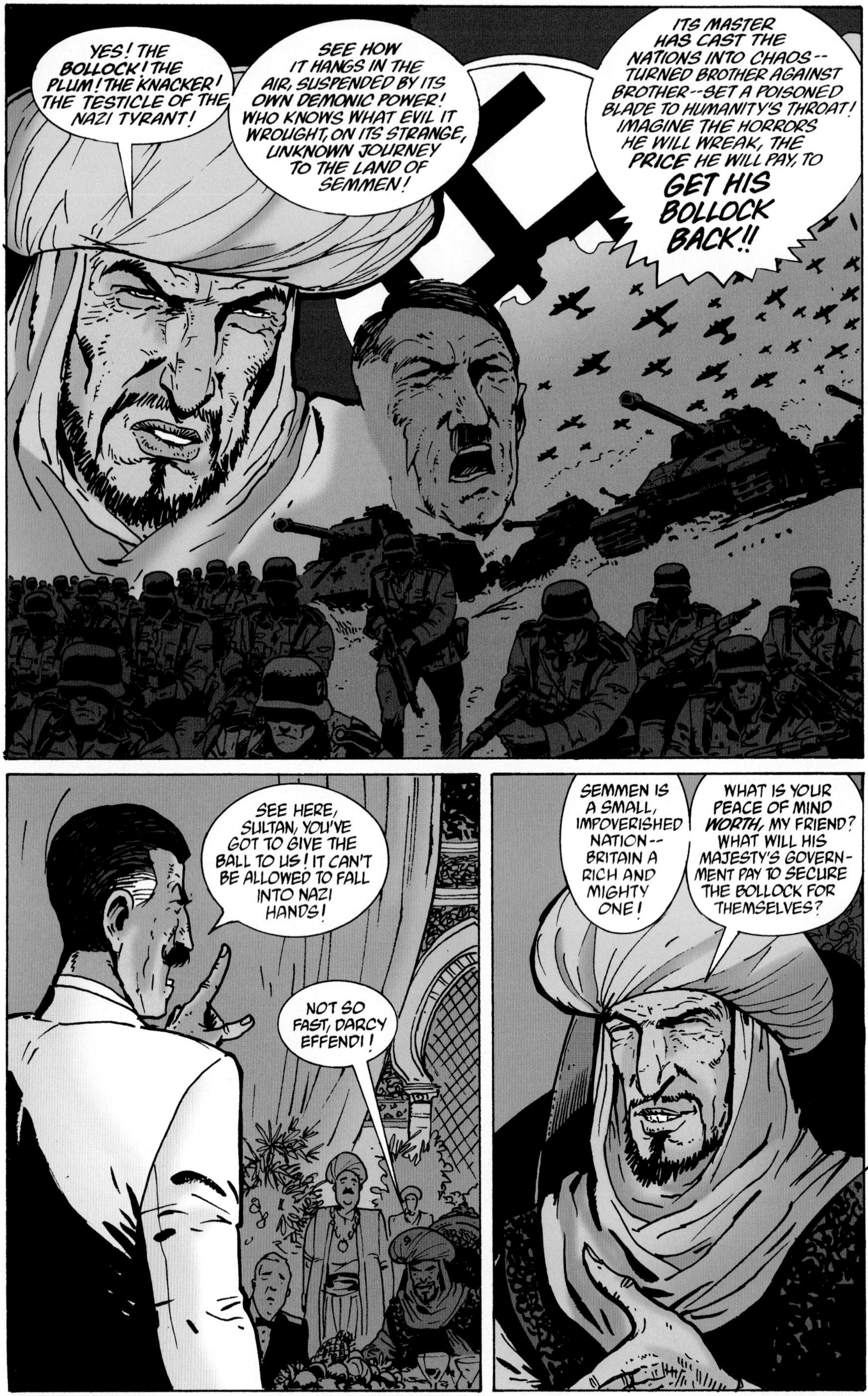

YES! THE BOLLOCK! THE PLUM! THE KNACKER! THE TESTICLE OF THE NAZI TYRANT!
SEE HOW IT HANGS IN THE AIR, SUSPENDED BY ITS OWN DEMONIC POWER! WHO KNOWS WHAT EVIL IT WROUGHT, ON ITS STRANGE, UNKNOWN JOURNEY TO THE LAND OF SEMMEN!
ITS MASTER HAS CAST THE NATIONS INTO CHAOS--TURNED BROTHER AGAINST BROTHER--SET A POISONED BLADE TO HUMANITY'S THROAT! IMAGINE THE HORRORS HE WILL WREAK, THE PRICE HE WILL PAY, TO GET HIS BOLLOCK BACK!!

SEE HERE, SULTAN, YOU'VE GOT TO GIVE THE BALL TO US! IT CAN'T BE ALLOWED TO FALL INTO NAZI HANDS!
NOT SO FAST, DARCY EFFENDI!

SEMMEN IS A SMALL, IMPOVERISHED NATION--BRITAIN A RICH AND MIGHTY ONE!
WHAT IS YOUR PEACE OF MIND WORTH, MY FRIEND? WHAT WILL HIS MAJESTY'S GOVERNMENT PAY TO SECURE THE BOLLOCK FOR THEMSELVES?

THE CRAFTY BLIGHTER! NEXT THING YOU KNOW HE'LL BRING THE YANKS AND THE HUNS IN, AND WE'LL ALL BE BIDDING FOR THE BLOODY THING!
BETTER GET OUR OFFER IN FIRST THEN, SIR!
WHILE YOU ARE DELIBERATING--SOME ENTERTAINMENT!
THE WOMEN OF MY ROYAL HAREM!
GAZE IN WONDER AS THESE GODDESSES PERFORM THE EXOTIC DANCES OF FABULOUS AND SENSUOUS ARABIA!
I SAY!
TH-THESE LADIES ARE IN A PARTIAL STATE OF UNDRESS, SIR--!
WHEN IN ROME, DOUBTFUL! NOTHING WRONG WITH A SPOT OF FOREIGN TOTTY, SO LONG AS IT'S IN MODERATION!
WHY, I REMEMBER ONCE IN THE SUDAN--GOOD GOD, THERE'S A WELL-UPHOLSTERED YOUNG FILLY!
I SALUTE YOU, MADAM! HUZZAH!

...THERE WE WERE, CRAZED CECIL AND FLAKEY DICK AND MYSELF, AND BUGGER ME RIGID IF THIS NATIVE GEL DIDN'T ONLY HAVE ONE KNEE...
JUST A MOMENT--
OH, CRIKEY! THE BOLLOCK, SIR!
THE BOLLOCK'S GONE!

BY ALLAH'S RINGPIECE! TREACHERY! TREACHERY!
BUT WHO COULD HAVE--
WHERE'S THAT HEFTILY-BOSOMED BINT GONE...?

THERE! AFTER HER, CHAPS!

LOOKS LIKE THE DUNGEON'S DOWN HERE, SIR!
FASTER, ALL OF YOU! WE CAN'T LET HER GET AWAY!

GAWD DAMMIT!
YER AHT OF ORDAH!
EY-OOP!
GOOD GOD ALMIGHTY--!

GERTA GASCH!!

INDEED!

THE RIFLE BRIGADE HAS FAILED! SOON I, GERTA GASCH, WILL STAND BEFORE THE FUHRER-- HIS GENITAL IN MY HANDS!
SOON I WILL HAVE MY LONG-DESERVED REWARD!
SPIT OR SWALLOW

YOU HAVEN'T WON YET, YOU SADISTIC SLATTERN! NOT 'TIL THE BALL IS BACK IN ADOLF'S SAC!
SILENCE!

HOW DARE YOU SPEAK OF OUR GLORIOUS LEADER'S UNDERCARRIAGE! ITS VERY MENTION IS AN INSULT IN YOUR FILTHY ENGLISH MOUTH!
ESPECIALLY YOURS, HUGO DARCY! YOU AND YOUR SPAZMO COMMANDOS HAVE BEEN A THORN IN THE SIDE OF THE REICH FOR FAR TOO LONG!

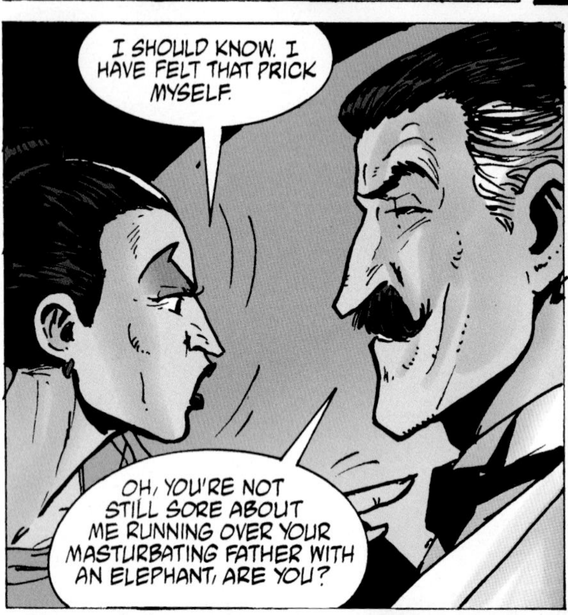
I SHOULD KNOW. I HAVE FELT THAT PRICK MYSELF.
OH, YOU'RE NOT STILL SORE ABOUT ME RUNNING OVER YOUR MASTURBATING FATHER WITH AN ELEPHANT, ARE YOU?

YOU SCHWEINE! YOU HAVE NO IDEA OF THE PAIN YOU HAVE CAUSED ME!

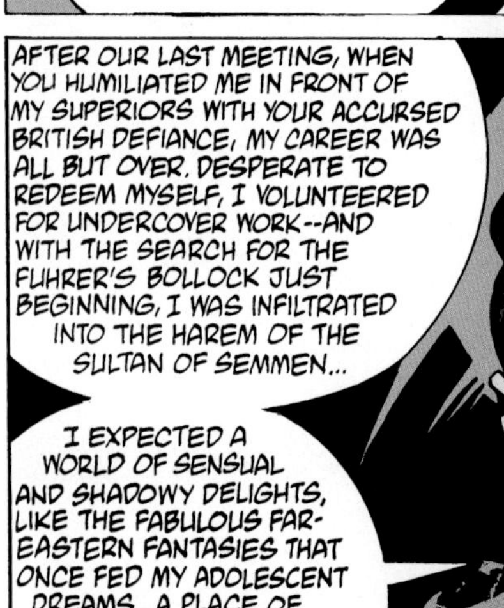
AFTER OUR LAST MEETING, WHEN YOU HUMILIATED ME IN FRONT OF MY SUPERIORS WITH YOUR ACCURSED BRITISH DEFIANCE, MY CAREER WAS ALL BUT OVER. DESPERATE TO REDEEM MYSELF, I VOLUNTEERED FOR UNDERCOVER WORK--AND WITH THE SEARCH FOR THE FUHRER'S BOLLOCK JUST BEGINNING, I WAS INFILTRATED INTO THE HAREM OF THE SULTAN OF SEMMEN...
I EXPECTED A WORLD OF SENSUAL AND SHADOWY DELIGHTS, LIKE THE FABULOUS FAR-EASTERN FANTASIES THAT ONCE FED MY ADOLESCENT DREAMS...A PLACE OF VEILS, WHICH, WHEN SWEPT ASIDE, WOULD REVEAL THE FORBIDDEN EROTIC MYSTERIES OF ANCIENT ARABIA...

AND DO YOU KNOW WHAT I GOT...?
COCK.

COCK, COCK, ARAB COCK! COCK FOR BREAKFAST, COCK FOR LUNCH AND COCK FOR FUCKING DINNER!
REALLY?

THREE MONTHS I'VE BEEN ON MY KNEES AND SPITTING CHEESE--ALL BECAUSE THAT ARSEHOLE OF A SULTAN STARTED DROPPING HINTS HE HAD THE BOLLOCK!
THAT MUST HAVE COME AS A BLOW.
AND EUNUCHS! HAVE YOU EVER TRIED TALKING TO A EUNUCH?
IT'S BORING!

HELLO, BORK, HOW ARE YOU TODAY? THEY TOOK MY DICK. ANOTHER BEAUTIFUL SUNSET, EH, KONGO? THEY TOOK MY DICK. HEY, RAKIM, FANCY A GAME OF SCRABBLE? AND SO ON AND SO ON AND FUCKING SO ON!
YOU ENGLANDER BASTARDS GOT ME THREE MONTHS IN HELL!

LOOK HERE, IT'S NOT OUR FAULT YOU WERE UP TO YOUR EYEBALLS IN TODGER--
OH, BUT IT IS, CAPTAIN. AND I INTEND TO PAY THE RIFLE BRIGADE BACK IN KIND.

SNIP.
SNIP.
SNIP.

EY-OOP!
GAWD DAMMIT!
YER AHT OF ORDAH!
YOU CAN'T BE SERIOUS, WOMAN!

I'M AFRAID SHE MOST DEFINITELY IS, CAPTAIN DARCY...
CARRINGTON-SHYTE! THEY GOT YOU AS WELL, EH?

WE GOT HIM SOME TIME AGO, CAPTAIN.
INDEED. IT WASN'T ALL ARAB COCK, YOU KNOW.
WAS IT... DARLING?

AGGLE
AGGLE
AGGLE
AGGLE
AGGLE
YOU FIENDS--!

THAT WAS AGAINST ALL THE RULES OF CIVILIZED WARFARE!
SO IT WAS YOU ALL ALONG, CARRINGTON-SHYTE! YOU TIPPED THIS SHE-DEVIL OFF WE WERE COMING--WHAT SORT OF AN ENGLISHMAN ARE YOU?!

THE TREACHEROUS SORT, OF COURSE...
THE SENSIBLE SORT! FOR WHAT IS ENGLAND COMPARED TO THE PROMISE OF A FORTUNE IN GERMAN GOLD--AND BLOW-JOBS?
THE DAY IS MINE, ENGLANDERS! THE BOLLOCK IS BOUND FOR BERLIN--AND ONCE REUNITED WITH ITS SCROTAL SIBLING, ITS INFERNAL POWER WILL SPREAD ACROSS THE WORLD!

WITHIN A MONTH THE WAR WILL BE OVER! WITHIN A YEAR THE RULE OF THE THIRD REICH WILL BE *TOTAL*!

THE SUPREMACY OF *ADOLF HITLER'S BALL* WILL ECLIPSE THE UNITED STATES--THE BOLSHEVIK RABBLE IN THE EAST--AND ALL WHO DARE OPPOSE US! THE SUN WILL FINALLY SET ON THE BRITISH EMPIRE...

WHAT RISES WILL BE SOMETHING ELSE ENTIRELY!

QUIET, YOU FOOLS! THE SULTAN MUST NOT DISCOVER OUR PRESENCE HERE--NOT BEFORE I RENDEZVOUS WITH THE AIRCRAFT THAT WILL TAKE ME TO BERLIN!
AND THAT BIG-HEADED LUFTWAFFE FUCKWIT HAD BETTER BE ON TIME...
THE RIFLE BRIGADE'S WEAPONS, FRAULEIN GASCH.

QUITE A LITTLE ARSENAL... KNIVES, HANDGUNS, DYNAMITE...A GRENADE OR TWO...
AND THE PIPES, OF COURSE.
WHAT PIPES, FRAULEIN?

DONNERWETTER! YOU LEFT THE PIPER HIS PIPES?!
PIPER-- TARTAN HELMET!

NEE-NAR-NEE-NO-NO-NAR-NAR
AAAHH! AAAAHHH!
AAAAAHHH!!

NO·NEE·NO·NAR·
NEE·NEE
NOT LONG NOW, CHAPS!
POIK
POIK
AAAIIII

RRRIPP
IIIEEE!
JUST THE TICKET! SEIZE THEIR GUNS!

EY-OOP!
GAWD DAMMIT!
YER AHT OF ORDAH!
SHOOT THEM ON SIGHT! NO MERCY! DON'T EVEN LET THEM GET OFF A--

COME ON THE RIFLE BRIGADE!
VERDAMMT, VERDAMMT!

SO, ONCE MORE FATE DELIVERS THE RIFLE BRIGADE INTO MY HANDS--BUT THIS TIME SHALL BE THE LAST!

THIS I SWEAR ON THE MEMORY OF MY BELOVED BROTHER--

HORRIDO! HORRIDO! *VENGEANCE IS MINE!*

DONNER UND BLITZEN! NEVER HAVE I SEEN SUCH ACCURATE SHOOTING!

TIME I WASN'T HERE!

AAIIEE! FIRST THE BOLLOCK IS STOLEN--NOW ALL HELL BREAKS LOOSE!
TO ARMS, MY WARRIORS!
AT YOUR COMMAND, O SULTAN!

THOSE LIMEY ASSHOLES'VE STIRRED UP A HORNETS' NEST! LOOKS LIKE THIS COULD BE MY CHANCE!

MY RIDE HOME! I KNEW THAT JAGDFLIEGER SCHEISSKOPF WOULD FUCK IT UP!
RATHER A SMALL PLANE TO CARRY BOTH OF US, WOULDN'T YOU SAY, DARLING...?

NEVER MIND THAT, YOU FOOL! HOW AM I GOING TO GET THE BOLLOCK OUT OF HERE NOW?

KISS MY ASS, WURST-SUCKER! MARYLAND SMITH STRIKES AGAIN!
TEUFEL!

IT DON'T PAY TO MESS WITH THE U.S. OF A., LIMPDICKS! NOW--HOME FOR GUM AN' PUSSY!
BRING DOWN THAT AIRCRAFT! OPEN FIRE!

AMMUNITION'S EXHAUSTED, SIR!
OF ALL THE BLASTED LUCK--!
HOW VERY INTERESTING, ENGLANDERS...

WHO THE--?
I SAY! THIS CHAP LOOKS ALMOST--FAMILIAR!
AND SO I SHOULD, HERR MILK...

FOR I AM *OBERLEUTNANT ERNST FLASCHMANN*-- DASHING FIGHTER ACE -- TERROR OF THE LADIES -- AND BROTHER OF THE SLIGHTLY LESS FAMOUS *OTTO*, THE PANZER HERO YOU KILLED IN BERLIN!
I MUST CONGRATULATE YOU ON DOWNING MY MACHINE, BUT IT WILL DO YOU LITTLE GOOD. I CAME HERE IN SEARCH OF JUSTICE FOR THE DEATH OF MY BROTHER--
--AND JUSTICE IS WHAT I SHALL HAVE!

HAVE YOU ANYTHING TO SAY BEFORE I DO WHAT I MUST...?
YOU CAN BALLY WELL *FUCK OFF*, FRITZ! I WOULDN'T GIVE YOU THE SATISFACTION!
W-W-WAIT A MINUTE--!

WE *HAD* TO KILL YOUR BROTHER! HE WAS AN *ENEMY SOLDIER*, WHAT *ELSE* WERE WE SUPPOSED TO DO?

...ACH, THIS WAR.
THIS...MADNESS THAT MEN INFLICT ON ONE ANOTHER.

YOU ARE SOLDIERS--OF COURSE YOU HAD TO DO YOUR DUTY. JUST AS I HAVE ALWAYS DONE MINE.
BUT SINCE MY BROTHER'S DEATH, I HAVE LET DUTY TURN TO HATRED. I HAVE LET THIS INSANE DESIRE FOR VENGEANCE EAT AT MY HEART LIKE A CANCER, UNTIL I WAS EVEN MORE OF A MINDLESS KILLER THAN THE NAZIS I HAVE ALWAYS LOATHED.
I FORGOT THAT--WE ARE ALL BROTHERS IN WAR. WE ARE ALL COM-RADES-IN-ARMS BENEATH OUR UNI-FORMS.

I SALUTE YOU, CAPTAIN DARCY! AND LIEUTENANT MILK...SERGEANT CRUMB... CORPORAL GEEZER...THE PIPER...HANKEN YANKEN...
GAWD DAMMIT!

IT IS GOOD TO KNOW WE PART, NOT AS ENEMIES--BUT AS FELLOW SOLDIERS.
AND PERHAPS, AFTER THE WAR...

WE SHALL SEE.
AUF WIEDERSEHEN.

BLAM
LET'S NOT GET SENTIMENTAL, FRITZ!
ALL BROTHERS IN WAR INDEED! WHAT *ABSOLUTE* ROT!

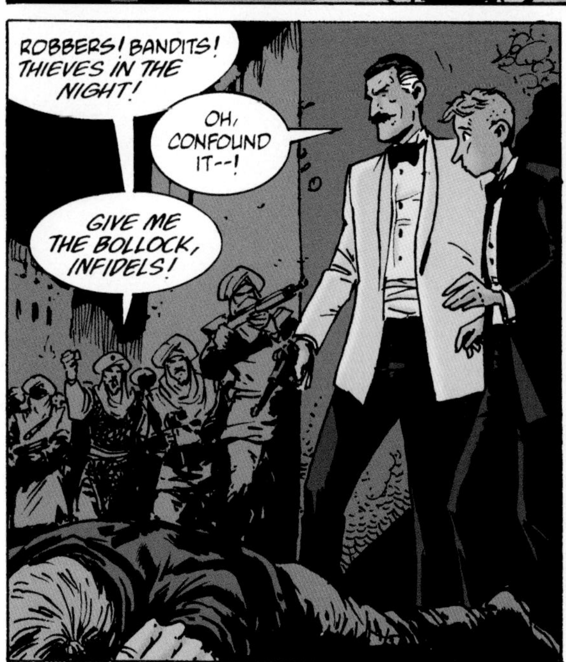
ROBBERS! BANDITS! *THIEVES IN THE NIGHT!*
OH, CONFOUND IT--!
GIVE ME THE BOLLOCK, INFIDELS!

LET'S SEE THOSE MONGOLOIDS TALK THEIR WAY OUT OF THIS ONE!
BE SURE TO PAY ATTENTION, MY DEAR. YOU'LL NEED TO KNOW HOW IT'S DONE.

WHAT?
THIS, I'M AFRAID, IS WHERE WE PART COMPANY. AS A REPRESENTATIVE OF THE FOREIGN OFFICE I HAVE FULL DIPLOMATIC IMMUNITY--WHEREAS YOU HAVE BUGGER ALL.
I'LL JUST CONDEMN YOU AND THE RIFLE BRIGADE AS CRIMINALS, STICK AROUND LONG ENOUGH TO SEE YOU ALL BEHEADED, AND BEETLE OFF BACK TO BLIGHTY WITH THE SULTAN NONE THE WISER...

YOU KLEINE SCHEISSE--!
THE AMERICAN, SIR! THE BLIGHTER'S COMING BACK!

TAKE US IN LOW, PETE! BE A SHAME TO GO HOME WITH-OUT GIVIN' THEM LIMEYS THE OL' BLUE MOON!
YOU GOT IT, BOSS!

...WHAT THE FUCK IS THAT?
FNARP

AH, THAT'S JUST MY PET BADGER, KEITH!
I HATE BADGERS, PETE! I HATE THE FUCKING THINGS!
GOMP

AAAAH! AAAHH! OH JESUS FUCKING CHRIST, GET IT AWAY FROM ME!
SHOW A LITTLE BACKBONE, WILL YOU?
WHAT ARE THEY DOING UP THERE...?

NO IDEA WHATSOEVER, SULTAN--
BUT THEY'RE THE ONES WITH THE BOLLOCK.

THE FUCKER'S COMIN' FOR ME! NO! NO! CAN'T LET IT HAPPEN!
WILLIP
YOU UNBELIEVABLE ASSHOLE, YOU'RE GONNA HIT THE--

FUEL...!

IS THAT--?
IT... LOOKS LIKE...
MEIN GOTT, IT CAN'T BE!

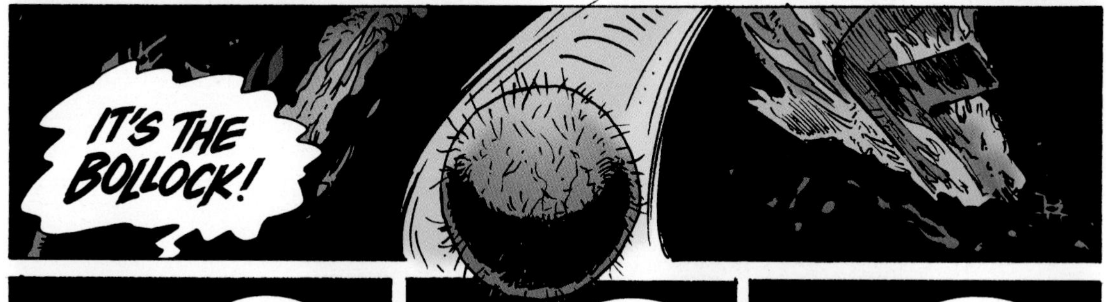
IT'S THE BOLLOCK!

GET IT!

GET IT!

GET IT!

EY-OOP!
GAWD DAMMIT!
YER AHT OF ORDAH!
THAT'S MY BOLLOCK, CAMEL-FUCKER!
NO, IT IS MINE-- AIIIEE!!
GOOD MAN, DOUBTFUL! ONE LAST EFFORT!
I CAN SEE IT, SIR!

I'VE GOT IT!
I'VE GOT IT!

GLOP

SS--
SS--!
AH... DOUBTFUL...?

DOUBTFUL OLD CHAP, SPEAK UP! WHAT ON EARTH'S THE MATTER WITH YOU?
SsSSs--

SIEG HEIL!

SIEG HEIL! SIEG HEIL! DER REICH VILL LAST VUN SOUSAND YEARS!
AAIEE! HE HAS BEEN POSSESSED BY THE MALIGN INFLUENCE OF THE BOLLOCK!
PULL YOURSELF TOGETHER, MAN!
SOON VUN OF US VILL BREAK--UND IT VILL NOT BE NATIONAL SOCIALIST CHERMANY!

BEND OVER, EVA! I VISH TO YANK OFF VILE YOU SPREAD YOUR ARSECHEEKS!
GIVE ME THAT, YOU FOOL!

TURN AROUND, HUGO DARCY! FACE ME!
WHAT THE BLAZES--?
THE BOLLOCK IS GONE--BUT AT LEAST I WILL HAVE MY REVENGE!

FOR THE DEATH OF MY FATHER! FOR WEEK UPON WEEK OF FLY-RIDDEN, CHEDDAR-SMEARED DONG! FOR TURNING MY MISSION INTO A FARCE!
ON YOUR KNEES AND SAY YOUR PRAYERS, YOU FILTHY ENGLANDER SCHWEINE-HUND!

FIRE AWAY, YOU DREARY JERRY HUSSY! "KHYBER" DARCY KNEELS TO NO ONE!
I SAY...!

LOOKS LIKE THE LITTLE FELLOW'S BITTEN OFF MORE THAN HE CAN CHEW...
AAACCCHH-- GAAK--

BLLOOOOORRRT

BLOORT BLOORT BLOORT
GOOD GOD! A FOUL EMISSION OF STEAMING BLACK MAN-FAT!
TAKE COVER!

GAH--!
BLOORT

AIIEEE!
BLOORT

AAAAAA GULK!
BLOORT

SARN'T CRUMB! SUBDUE THAT OFFICER!

EY-OOP!
UHH--!
STOUT FELLOW!

TRIFLE TOO LATE FOR THESE CHAPS, MIND YOU. GAD, WHAT A DREADFUL WAY TO GO...

STILL, CAN'T BE HELPED.
RIGHT! BACK TO THE EMBASSY, A GALLON OF CASTOR OIL FOR THE LIEUTENANT, AND WE'LL WAIT FOR THE BOLLOCK TO COME OUT THE OTHER END-- THEN IT'S HOME WE JOLLY WELL GO!

YER AHT OF ORDAH...!
I'VE BEEN WONDERING ABOUT THAT TOO, CORPORAL. HOW DID WE ALONE RESIST THE GHASTLY EFFECT THAT HITLER'S KNACKER HAD ON THESE OTHER POOR SOULS?
D'YOU KNOW WHAT I THINK...?

THEY JUST WEREN'T BRITISH ENOUGH.
OMMMM

BLIGHTY:
SHERRY?
ABSOLUTELY...

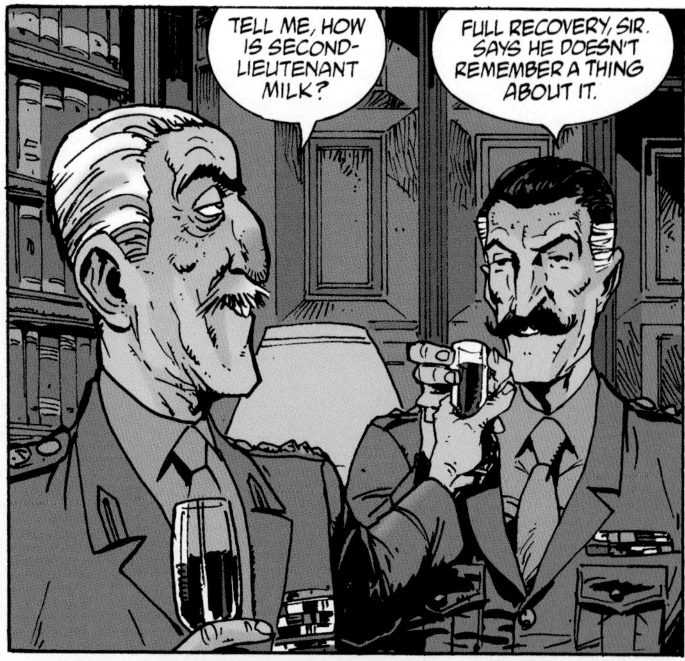
TELL ME, HOW IS SECOND-LIEUTENANT MILK?
FULL RECOVERY, SIR. SAYS HE DOESN'T REMEMBER A THING ABOUT IT.

UTTERLY WIZARD SHOW YOU AND YOUR CHAPS PUT ON, HUGO. GONGS ALL 'ROUND, I SHOULDN'T WONDER.
CHIN-CHIN!
ONE THING DOES PUZZLE ME, SIR...

WHAT WILL BE DONE WITH THE BOLLOCK NOW?

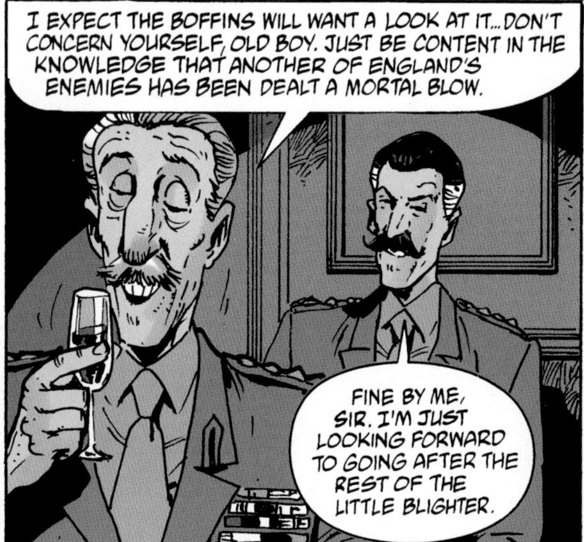
I EXPECT THE BOFFINS WILL WANT A LOOK AT IT...DON'T CONCERN YOURSELF, OLD BOY. JUST BE CONTENT IN THE KNOWLEDGE THAT ANOTHER OF ENGLAND'S ENEMIES HAS BEEN DEALT A MORTAL BLOW.
FINE BY ME, SIR. I'M JUST LOOKING FORWARD TO GOING AFTER THE REST OF THE LITTLE BLIGHTER.

OH, HIS TIME IS COMING, HUGO. WE'LL GET OLD ADOLF ONE OF THESE DAYS...

BUT POOR OL' GOEBBELS, 'AS NO BALLS, AT ALL... ♪

THE Rifle Brigade WILL RETURN!*

*THEN AGAIN...

GARTH ENNIS

HAS BEEN WRITING COMICS FOR OVER TWENTY-FIVE YEARS. HIS CREDITS INCLUDE *PREACHER, THE BOYS, HITMAN, RED TEAM, CALIBAN, ROVER RED CHARLIE, BATTLEFIELDS* AND *WAR STORIES*. ORIGINALLY FROM BELFAST, NORTHERN IRELAND, ENNIS NOW LIVES IN NEW YORK CITY WITH HIS WIFE, RUTH.

CARLOS EZQUERRA

HAS BEEN DRAWING COMICS FOR FORTY-FIVE YEARS. HE IS THE CREATOR AND DESIGNER OF *JUDGE DREDD, STRONTIUM DOG, MAJOR EAZY, JUST A PILGRIM, CURSED EARTH KOBURN, ADVENTURES IN THE RIFLE BRIGADE, RAT PACK, AL'S BABY*, AND MANY MORE. BORN IN SPAIN, HE CURRENTLY LIVES IN ANDORRA, RIGHT IN THE HEART OF THE PYRENEES.

ALSO AVAILABLE FROM IMAGE COMICS

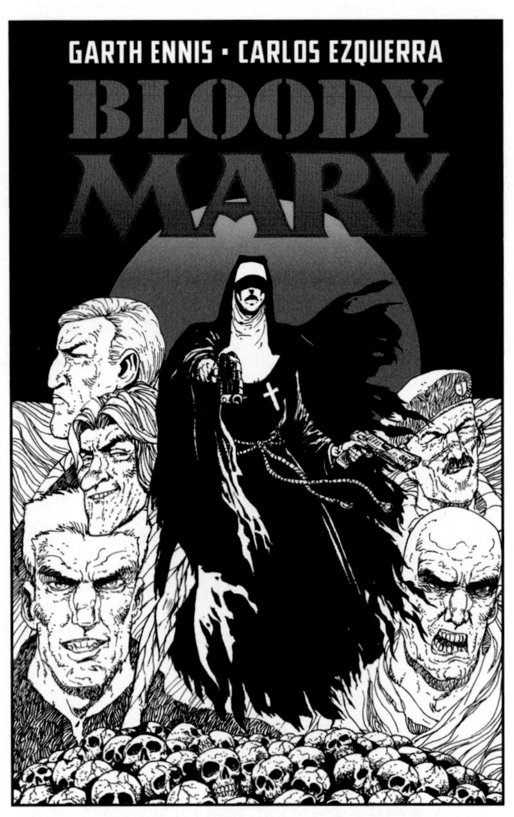

IN 1999, WE ALL WENT BACK TO WAR

In a reality even worse than our own, a third great European conflict has dragged the major powers into a catastrophic war of attrition. Whole nations are ruined, with the death toll running into many millions. Now Mary Malone, the most dangerous assassin in a world of killers, finds herself set against adversaries whose evil insanity knows no bounds.

Together with her sidekick the Major—delusional but deadly—Mary must face both a man who cannot die and a crazed cult leader whose flock are all too ready to die for him. Garth Ennis *(Preacher, The Boys, War Story)* and Carlos Ezquerra *(Judge Dredd, Strontium Dog, Adventures in the Rifle Brigade)* present an action-packed tale of future warfare—and a heroine whose faith lies firmly in firepower.

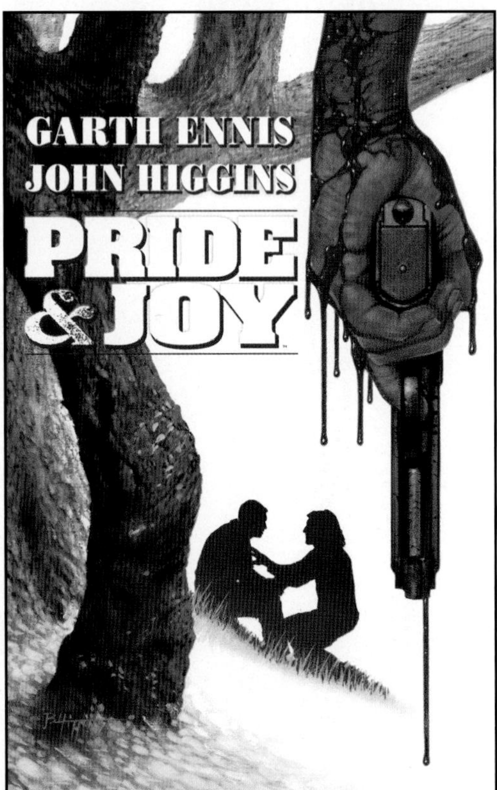

SOME DEBTS CAN ONLY BE PAID IN BLOOD

Still mourning the loss of his wife, Jimmy Kavanagh lives quietly in the backwoods of New England, raising his devoted daughter and resentful teenage son. But fate has come calling in the worst possible way, as Jimmy's criminal past threatens to destroy his entire family—raising the spectre of his crushing guilt for an old and awful crime.

On the run with a pair of unwanted associates from long ago, Jimmy and his children are pursued by a foe so ruthless and lethal that no one will stand between him and his prey. A showdown is inevitable—but does Jimmy still have what it takes to fight for his family's survival? And will his horror at his own transgressions consume him long before the predator on his trail?

Garth Ennis *(Preacher, Crossed, Battlefields)* and John Higgins *(Judge Dredd, Razorjack, War Story)* present a hard-boiled tale of a man at bay—whose only hope of redemption lies on a dark and bloody path.